SHEENA WILKINSON

HOPE *against* HOPE

Little Island

HOPE AGAINST HOPE

First published in 2020 by
Little Island
7 Kenilworth Park
Dublin 6W, Ireland
www.littleisland.ie

A British Library Cataloguing in Publication record for this book is available
from the British Library.

Cover illustration and design by Niall McCormack
Typeset by Kieran Nolan
Proofread by Emma Dunne
Printed in Poland by Drukarnia Skleniarz

Print ISBN 978-1-912417-42-1
Ebook (Kindle) ISBN: 978-1-912417-62-9
Ebook (other platforms) ISBN: 978-1-912417-63-6

Little Island receives financial assistance from
The Arts Council/An Chomhairle Ealaíon

10 9 8 7 6 5 4 3 2 1

For Emma Campbell, with love

*If the friendships at Helen's Hope endure
as well as ours, they'll be lucky girls indeed*

Historical Note

The island of Ireland has been divided, since 1921, into two separate states: Northern Ireland and what is today called the Republic of Ireland. Northern Irish society is split between mainly Protestant 'unionists', who want to remain part of the United Kingdom, and mainly Catholic 'nationalists', who want to join with the Republic to form a united Ireland. There are also many people in Northern Ireland who do not identify strongly with either of these positions. *Hope against Hope* is set during 1921, just as the island was about to be partitioned into these two states by a border which is still politically contested today.

Ireland in 1921 was in a state of bloody war and political turmoil. For many years Ireland had been ruled directly from Britain, but many people wanted independence, especially after an armed rebellion known as the Easter Rising in 1916. Sinn Féin, who triumphed in the 1918 General Election, declared an Irish republic in 1919, with its own parliament, the Dáil (pronounced 'dawl'), in Dublin, but this was not accepted by the British government. The Irish Republican Army began waging war against Britain in 1919. This war is known as the Anglo-Irish War or the War of Independence. Britain retaliated by sending a very brutal force known as the 'Black and Tans' to Ireland to back up the police. There were terrible atrocities on both sides.

In December 1920, the British government passed the Government of Ireland Act, which allowed Ireland a limited form of independence known as Home Rule. However, this did not satisfy those who wanted an independent republic, completely free from Britain. The Government of Ireland Act involved partitioning the island into two, Northern Ireland and Southern Ireland. Elections for the two new parliaments (north and south) were held in May 1921. Sinn Féin rejected the Government of Ireland Act, and when they won a landslide victory south of the border, they did not take their seats in the new Dublin parliament, but sat instead in the Dáil, and the war continued.

In the north, unionists, who wanted to remain part of the United Kingdom, initially were not happy with the Act either. They wanted to continue to be ruled from London. The Ulster Unionist Party won forty of the fifty-two seats in the elections to the new Belfast parliament and were determined to resist any attempts to weaken the union with Britain. Northern nationalists, on the other hand, hated partition and feared for their rights in this new state, which had come into being against a background of intense sectarian violence.

Just after the events described in *Hope against Hope*, in July 1921, a truce was called to try to end the Anglo-Irish War, which was finally brought to an end by the Anglo-Irish Treaty in December, and the Irish Free State (today the Republic of Ireland) was established. However, this compromise proved unacceptable to many nationalists and led to further violence in the Irish Civil War.

The border was always seen as a temporary solution. In fact, it was hoped by both Britain and by Irish nationalists that the two parts of Ireland would eventually be reunited under a Dublin parliament. Yet the border on the island of Ireland remains a highly contentious issue to this day, particularly since the recent British decision to leave the European Union.

The city of Belfast has always been prone to outbreaks of sectarian violence. This violence was especially intense in 1921. Then, as during the more recent Northern Ireland Troubles and even today, many good people worked hard to establish better community relations and break down traditional barriers, but often these attempts have been met with resistance, as the girls in the story find out.

Irish history is full of contradictions, complications and compromises, and never more so than in 1921. It was a terrible time, and the characters' hopes for a brighter future would not be realised for many years. But throughout all those years, there have always been brave people like Polly and Stella and their friends, trying their best to keep hope alive.

Sheena Wilkinson
November 2019

Chapter 1

FLORA GALBRAITH was in our shop! Buying undies! At least her mother was buying; Flora was eyeing the shelves of old-lady nighties and boxes of men's handkerchiefs (*Ideal Gift!*) and sighing.

Daddy was showing Flora's mother McCabe's best 'Junior Miss' range.

'Of course you'll appreciate the quality, Mrs Galbraith,' he said, unfolding a flannel petticoat and running his hands down it. 'See how sturdy the seams are?'

I got the giggles seeing Daddy's big hands on a girl's petticoat. I was meant to be seen-and-not-heard behind the counter writing labels – *Ideal Gift!*; *Baby's Layette*; *Chil-Prufe Vests On Special Offer!* I normally hated our shop, it was the most boring place in Mullankeen – which is saying quite a lot – but my brother Leo was having one of what Daddy called his 'spells'. Catherine, my cousin, lived next door, but for some reason Auntie May didn't want me there today, so Daddy had dragged me to the shop out of the way. I'd protested loudly that I was fifteen, not a baby, but I was secretly relieved. When Leo had one of his

1

spells he was scary, shouting and roaring, which was bad, or crying, which was worse.

I caught Flora's eye and grinned, hoping I wasn't blushing. We didn't exactly know the Galbraiths – they were posh and Protestant and lived in Lismore, a big stone house on the Armagh Road – but I had had a secret kinship with Flora since I was twelve. So secret that she didn't know about it. Three years ago, at the Christmas fête in the Church of Ireland, I had bought ten books – school stories by Angela Brazil – and they were all marked neatly inside with her name. They had titles like *The Luckiest Girl in the School* and *A Popular Schoolgirl*.

I fell in love with the stories. Even the pictures were intoxicating: fine, detailed line drawings, all of girls. All the girls were pretty and all the girls were having fun. Girls in classrooms, girls on ponies, girls laughing with their arms round each other, girls running after a ball with what looked like hurling sticks but I soon found out were hockey sticks, girls girls girls. A world of girls. A world away from Mullankeen and the shop and Leo, and me having to do everything at home, and people talking all the time about the border and partition and what would become of us all.

Lucky Flora looked like the girls in the stories – all pout and profile and, very daring for Mullankeen in 1921, her dark hair neatly bobbed. Last time I saw her she'd had two plaits flying out behind her when she cantered along the lanes on her grey pony, Moonshine.

'I like your hair,' I said shyly now.

Flora tossed her head and the dark bob swung round

and fell neatly back into place. I sighed with envy. My hair looked like a very angry ginger mop. It hadn't always; Mammy used to help me keep it nice.

'It's for school,' she said.

'*Boarding* school?' I could hardly keep the envy out of my voice.

She nodded gloomily. 'Next week. Some ghastly seminary for young ladies called Ellis House. I keep hoping there'll be some terrible riot or something up in Belfast to scare my parents off, but it's depressingly civilised around Ellis House, apparently.' She even *sounded* like the girls in the books.

'I'd love to go to boarding school.' I considered saying that I had read all her cast-off stories, but didn't want to sound babyish.

Flora's mother and Daddy looked up. As usual I must have been too loud. I was always getting told off for it.

'Polly,' Daddy said in a warning voice, 'I hope you aren't annoying Miss Galbraith.'

'Not at all,' Flora's mother said, as if Flora couldn't answer for herself. 'It sounds as if your daughter has a most sensible attitude.' She beamed at me. I wasn't used to being called sensible. 'Flora's being very silly about leaving home,' Mrs Galbraith went on.

Flora looked mulish. 'You shouldn't have dismissed McMahon,' she muttered. 'I can't trust anyone else to look after Moonshine.'

Jamie McMahon was the groom and general outdoor servant up at Lismore. He was sweet on Catherine; I'd seen him looking at her at Mass.

'Why was Jamie –?' I started to ask.

'Polly.' Daddy's warning voice again. 'Don't interrupt, and hurry up with those labels. I want to change the window display this afternoon for Easter. Now, Mrs Galbraith, a dozen pairs of navy?'

Mrs Galbraith frowned at the list in her hand. 'Yes, please,' she said. 'Such a relief that you have them – we ordered them from the school uniform supplier, but they've let us down and I can't send her off to school with no – er – underthings.'

'Well, now you know where we are, you can always get what you need here in McCabe's.' This was Daddy's sneaky way of saying that the Galbraiths had never darkened our door before: the shop was in Main Street in Mullankeen so they *can't* not have known where it was. 'You'll be anxious about her, up in the city.' Daddy wrapped the navy knickers in tissue paper and rummaged under the counter for brown paper to make a parcel.

'Yes. She was to go in September but she had measles, and then we were worried about the political situation. But the part where the school is is very quiet,' Mrs Galbraith said. 'Well away from any nonsense,' she went on, as if the riots and murders we read about in the newspaper were a playground scuffle between silly boys. She lowered her voice, though there was nobody else in the shop. 'As a matter of fact, I worry more about things round here. So many young hotheads around. And then this partition business puts us in such an awkward position – literally. Since my husband bought some more fields last year

4

Lismore straddles the county boundary, and now our land's in two different *countries*. Ridiculous.'

'Desperate indeed.' Daddy always agreed with customers. 'But sure it will all be sorted out in time. That border can't last.'

I squirmed inside as I always did when the conversation turned to politics, but, imprisoned by the counter, I couldn't escape. Flora had moved to the door and was waiting for her mother in ostentatious boredom, one hand on the handle.

'My niece Catherine is heading to Belfast soon too,' Daddy said.

I knew better than to exclaim aloud. But – Catherine? Belfast? I listened with fascinated horror, my pen poised over the next label.

'She's going to commercial college,' Daddy went on, 'to learn shorthand and typing.'

'Mother, please hurry,' Flora said from the doorway, hanging on the door handle. 'You promised me tea in the Singing Kettle and I'm going to expire with starvation.'

Mrs Galbraith shook her head. 'Girls!' she said. 'Always such drama. All right, darling, I'm coming.'

As soon as they had gone I turned to Daddy.

'What do you mean about Catherine?' I demanded. 'She can't go to Belfast! She'll be terrified. And she's never mentioned shorthand and typing. She'll be hopeless – she can hardly write, let alone type.' I wasn't being unkind, only truthful: Catherine got her letters back to front and jumbled up. But as well as bewildered I felt hurt.

5

Catherine was my best friend as well as my cousin. How could she be going to Belfast without telling me? Was this why Auntie May hadn't let me go to her house today?

And why wasn't *I* getting the chance to go to Belfast? Why was every other girl in the world luckier than me?

Daddy sighed. 'Shorthand and typing are useful,' he said. 'And Auntie May thinks she'd benefit from a change of scene. A change of company.'

'But where will she live?'

We had no relatives in Belfast, and I couldn't imagine Catherine living in lodgings. She was sixteen but she got tongue-tied in shops and stammered when she had to speak to strangers. 'The wee backward one', the gossipy women who hung around after Mass used to say, which Catherine hated, but they also called her 'the wee pretty one', which *I* hated. Mammy and Catherine's mother had been twins, and Catherine and I had both inherited their red curls, but Catherine's hair was silky and bouncy, whereas mine was always in what Mammy used to call a bee's wisp. Catherine had wide blue eyes like a kitten; mine were mud-coloured; Catherine had pale creamy skin; mine was freckled like a speckled egg. I had 'spirit', but people in Mullankeen didn't like spirit, except the holy sort.

'She's going to live in a girls' hostel,' Daddy said. 'Now that's enough about it, Polly. Finish those labels and be careful. You've blotted that one – you'll have to do it again. You're so careless. No wonder …' He sighed and sucked his moustache as if he didn't trust himself not to say something unpleasant.

Something like *No wonder Auntie May wants to send Catherine away from your bad influence.*

Since Mammy died I'd often felt a spiky black bud of anger inside me. Now it bloomed into a fierce flower. I threw the labels and pen on to the floor. Ink splattered everywhere.

'Polly!' Daddy cried, but I was already pushing up the folding bit of the counter and storming out of the shop.

Chapter 2

I STOMPED along Main Street with my head high, trying to ignore the tears flickering behind my eyes. Catherine was being sent away from me. People always said I would go to the bad. When I was wee I thought it was a place – The Bad, like the town square or the top field or the chapel – and it always sounded more exciting and exotic than anywhere around Mullankeen.

Leo used to stick up for me. 'Our Polly's only spirited,' he'd say whenever I was in trouble for starting a fight in the schoolyard or playing knock-the-doors-and-run at the big houses up Leonard's Hill or sneaking a storybook into Mass. He would ruffle my hair and call me Polly-wolly-doodle. Leo was seven years older than me, but when he came home from the war two years ago he seemed more like seventy years older, and a completely different person. I sort of hated Leo now. I knew I should be grateful he wasn't killed, but the real Leo seemed to have been replaced by a horrible stranger. Sometimes I wished that if one person in my family had had to die, it could have been Leo instead of Mammy. Most of the time he was silent, and when he did talk we ended up fighting.

If it weren't for Catherine I'd have been really lonely. It was all right at school, when all the children ran about together, but now I was fifteen and officially helping at home I was too respectable to giggle in the back lanes with the mill girls and maids, but too common for the Lennoxes and the Galbraiths with their posh voices and ponies. 'Helping' was a joke: I did everything now Mammy was dead, skivvying for two ungrateful men. I used to fantasise about running away and leaving them, but there was nowhere to go.

And now Catherine was escaping. Catherine was a goody-goody, scared of her mammy and the nuns and trouble, and she didn't like books and making things up and having adventures the way I did, but we'd always been friends. Mullankeen would be unbearable without her. No wonder I was upset!

Main Street gave way to the Newry Road, fringed with trees, bright with white blossom. Exactly half a mile to the end of our lane. But I walked past our house, and on over the wee humpy bridge, to the small whitewashed house where Catherine lived. Next door, but a whole county away! Catherine and I thought it was a great joke that we lived next door to each other but in different counties. Different *countries* now, because Armagh was in the new Northern Ireland and Monaghan was in what the British called Southern Ireland – but that was silly. How would they know where to draw the line on a map? The river – a stream really – was the county boundary, but where

9

would the border actually be? In the water? How would you know what was the exact middle? My head hurt when I thought about it. As for *Southern* Ireland, that was even more confusing, because Donegal was the most northerly county, and it wasn't in Northern Ireland.

There was only a hundred yards between our houses, and if I hung a signal out of my window – a red flag or something, the kind of thing girls in books were always doing – Catherine would have seen it plainly. We never did do that because Catherine said what was the point, if I wanted to see her I could just run up the road in less time than it would take to hang a flag out the window, and anyway where on earth would I get a flag? Catherine was sweet but not imaginative.

And now she was going away. Without me. She would be miles away in Belfast and I would have nobody. Only Daddy and Leo for ever and ever.

I didn't bother knocking; we always ran in and out of each other's houses, which was why I'd been so surprised that Auntie May didn't want me today. Catherine was in the kitchen, taking a batch of scones out of the oven. Even in a faded old striped apron, with heat from the oven pinking her cheeks, she looked pretty.

The scones smelt gorgeous, as Catherine's baking always did, but I didn't waste any time.

'Are you being sent away because of me?' I demanded. 'Because I'm a bad influence?'

'What?' Her cheeks flamed deeper in a way that was nothing to do with the heat of the oven. 'Don't be daft.'

'Daddy says Auntie May didn't like the company you were keeping.'

Catherine looked over her shoulder as if her mother was about to come in. 'She didn't mean you. Why do you always think everything's about you?'

'I don't!'

'I can't talk about it here. Come out for the eggs with me.'

She set the baking tray down, then grabbed an old basket from beside the back door. I followed her out to the scrubby patch at the end of the garden, scratched bare by the hens.

'So who is it, if it's not me?'

Catherine squatted and retrieved a brown egg from behind a clump of daisies.

'Jamie,' she said. 'Jamie McMahon.' Her face went daft-looking, what Mammy used to call 'saft'.

'Are you courting?'

She nodded. Then shook her head. 'I don't know,' she said. 'He meets me in the lane on his way home from work. He says I'm the prettiest girl in Mullankeen.'

'Well, you are.' Even Flora Galbraith wasn't as pretty as Catherine. 'Is that all? What a lot of fuss over nothing. Oh, my goodness! He hasn't tried to have his way with you, has he?' I wasn't sure exactly what that was, but I was fairly sure it was something to do with letting them put their hands up your skirts, and boys were mad for it but girls had to say no. It wasn't the kind of thing I could even imagine wanting to do. I thought about the girls in the school stories. Flora Galbraith and her dozen pairs of sturdy navy knickers. I couldn't see her having any truck with that kind of thing either.

'No! Don't be so disgusting.' But she blushed deeper and twisted her fingers together and sighed.

'Then what's the problem? Is it because he's a servant? Oh – but he's been dismissed, hasn't he? I heard that in the shop this morning.'

She bit her lip. 'You know his brother Tony's in the IRA?'

'So?' I was the last person to care what anyone's brother did. I knew the IRA were active in the war against England for Irish independence, and that lots of people in Mullankeen supported them. But we never got involved in politics: having a shop, we had to keep in with everyone. Of course a few people boycotted McCabe's because of Leo having served in the British army in the Great War – some people thought that made him a traitor to Ireland, but Daddy always said we didn't need their custom. I couldn't help agreeing with them, not because I understood the politics but because I could see how the war had wrecked Leo's life. And ours.

'So he's been lifted for the murder of that policeman last week. And people say Jamie helped him, only they can't prove anything. That's why the Galbraiths have dismissed him. That's why my parents want me to go away. They think I'm' – she frowned, searching for the right words – 'easily influenced.' She sighed. 'Poor Jamie. I wish I could help him.'

'Oh.' Catherine *was* easily influenced, but mostly by me. I didn't like to think of her in thrall to a young man, especially one who might be in the IRA. 'You'll hate Belfast,' I said. 'It's all riots and shootings.'

She shuddered. 'Mammy says the part I'm going to is very respectable. And I'm going to live in a hostel with other girls.' Even her curls seemed to droop at the prospect.

'It sounds horrible,' I said.

I didn't mean it. I was ferociously jealous. I wanted to escape from Mullankeen and being a skivvy! I wanted to live in a hostel with other girls. I was the adventurous one and I wasn't a bit scared of trouble.

'Why don't I come and keep you company?' I said. 'You'll be too shy on your own.' I saw us together in Belfast, me protecting Catherine, like I always did, and managing to have fun at the same time. A girls' hostel! Surely the next best thing to boarding school. I wouldn't even mind going to a commercial college. Imagine escaping from Leo and all the dusting and cooking and scrubbing! Imagine living somewhere with lots of girls instead of two men!

Catherine's creamy cheeks flooded with pink. 'Oh, Poll! I'd love you to come. But your daddy needs you. Sure you'd never leave him and your Leo.'

That was what it always came down to. That was why I would never get a chance to go anywhere. Because it was my duty to stay at home and look after the men. I imagined again those lines on the map, only this time they weren't marking the border; they were just closing in around me, making my world smaller and smaller.

Chapter 3

CATHERINE left after Easter and I sulked and fretted, especially because Flora had gone too. I didn't miss her like I missed Catherine, but I hadn't realised how much I'd relied on the odd glimpses I'd had of her, riding Moonshine round the lanes or driving with her daddy in their big Vauxhall motor car. I knew it was silly, having a sort of pash on her, but I couldn't help it.

I might as well have saved my energy: Daddy never noticed my sulks. And Leo never noticed me at all. He only wanted to sit in his room or go for long solitary walks in the lanes where you met nobody except sheep. And sometimes he walked away on out the Monaghan Road to an awful old shebeen of a place called Fox's where he bought whiskey. Catherine told me Jamie McMahon had seen him there. Daddy never asked him where he got the money for the whiskey but I knew: he withdrew his savings from the Ulster Bank in town and kept it in a sock under his mattress. I knew because I was the one who changed the beds. Once, after he'd had a very bad spell, I thought of taking the sock and hiding it, so he couldn't buy the whiskey, but I was too scared. Daddy never mentioned the drinking. Never scolded Leo or told him what a pain he was. There was no question of Leo being nagged to help in the shop, even when Daddy came home exhausted in the evenings. I knew why: people mightn't come to McCabe's if he was working there. They would go to McGrady's at the other end of town, even though the counters were dusty and there was a rumour that someone had bought a tablecloth there and when they opened the package there were mouse droppings in the folds. Whereas McCabe's, even without Mammy, was always clean.

As for Leo helping in the house, well, obviously nobody expected that.

Daddy came home late one evening looking exhausted, old and stooped and without a word to throw at a dog, not that we had a dog. Dinner was late and dry and we all sat and played with our food, pretending there was nothing wrong. I hated how we always did that. I set my fork down and said, my voice loud over the muted chewings and cutlery scrapings, 'What's wrong, Daddy?'

'Nothing, love. I'm just tired.'

'I could help in the shop,' I offered. The shop was boring but it would be better than cleaning and cooking.

'No,' Daddy said, more sharply than I'd ever heard him speak. 'You've enough to do here.' Then, more gently, 'I don't want you in the shop, especially after …' He shook his head. 'Never worry your head about it,' he said.

'About what?'

Daddy took a drink of water and wiped his mouth with his napkin. 'Och, a wee bit of trouble in the town.'

'What sort of trouble?'

'Graffiti – old nonsense.'

'Why would that make you late?'

Daddy hesitated. 'Well,' he said, 'I couldn't leave it, so I got to cleaning it off.'

'You mean it was on our shop?'

'It was probably wains.'

'What did it say?' I knew I was on dangerous ground. I could imagine what it said. I looked sideways at Leo but he was hunched over his plate, pushing bits of meat around and showing no interest at all.

'Nothing,' Daddy said.

'It can't have been very hard to clean off, if it said nothing.'

Leo jerked into life. 'Don't be cheeky, Polly,' he said. Three or four years ago, he would have said, 'Och, she's not cheeky, she's just funny.' I'd rather he stayed morose and silent than opened his mouth to tell me off.

I had one of my sharp kicks of hatred for my brother. He had come home from the war without a single scratch. Which made the way he carried on even more exasperating. Bad enough that he'd actually marched away in a British uniform to fight for the King, without him being such a grump. He never went into town, even to Mass, so he didn't hear what people muttered – *Traitor to Ireland. Fighting for bloody England.* I could well imagine what had been scrawled on the wall of our shop.

Of course Leo wasn't the only man from Mullankeen to have fought in the Great War. Flora Galbraith's older brother was killed, and two of the Lennox boys had fought. But they

16

were Protestants. And even though the war was over, now they were cutting Ireland in two and the border was pressing right against our house, and everywhere you went people were talking about war and guns and fighting. I could sort of understand Daddy not wanting me hanging round the town. There was an election coming soon, to see who would govern the new state of Northern Ireland. Around Mullankeen there was a lot of talk about boycotting the elections, not recognising the new state. I remembered Daddy saying to Mrs Galbraith that the border couldn't last anyway.

After the graffiti incident, home was even more depressing. The late April days were long and warm, but Leo's black moods sucked the light out of the house. What little light there was since Mammy died. We couldn't speak without fighting. Auntie May called in from time to time and told me to stay out of his way.

'You've plenty of housework to do,' she said, like this was meant to be a comfort.

'I hate housework. When I grow up I'm never going to do any.'

'Don't be childish, Polly. You'll be a wife some time, please God, and you need to learn how to run a home.'

'I don't want to be a wife.' I glared at the brass lamp-base she was making me shine. 'And I already know far more than I ever wanted to about running a home.'

But our house wasn't a home any more, and it was nothing to do with how dull the brasses were.

'You don't want to be a spinster, do you?'

Spinsters were women who couldn't get men. They knelt

muttering over their rosaries for ages after Mass, when everyone else was away out of the chapel like a lilty. Catherine used to whisper that they were praying for husbands, which always made me giggle because Miss O'Loane was as wide as a Mullingar heifer, and as hairy, and Miss Foley was about ninety and looked like a goblin. Miss McVey looked normal but she lived with her brother.

I imagined having to live with Leo for the rest of my life, even after Daddy died. Putting up with his moods, waiting anxiously for him to come home when he was on the batter. That wasn't what I wanted at all. I wanted to live in my own house, on my own, or maybe with a friend to share. To do what I wanted. But did girls get the chance to do that? I thought of Catherine, up in Belfast. Catherine wanted nothing better than to be someone's wife – though surely not Jamie McMahon's – and yet she was the one learning to be an office girl, and hating every minute of it, if her letters were anything to go by. If only we could swap places. I sighed. Even Flora Galbraith, who was rich and lucky, had been sent where she didn't want to go.

'The world's ill-divid,' I said, which Mammy used to say.

'Don't talk nonsense, Polly. And hurry up with that polishing.'

There was a letter from Catherine by the afternoon post. I'd escaped from the house and was swinging on the old tree-swing Leo had made me years ago, when the postman cycled down the lane. He handed me two letters, one for me addressed in Catherine's careful round-hand and one thin brown envelope addressed to Daddy, the kind that made him frown.

I read Catherine's letter, which made *me* frown, because she was so obviously unhappy.

Dear Polly

I supose I'm getting used to it heer. the shothand is still very hard I dont seme to get on with it atall. Typing is hard to you arent alowd to look at your hands your supost to remeber wehre the kees are & the teecher wraps your nuckels if you get to many wrods rong. Its not to bad in the hostle, the girls are nice aprt from a buly calld Ivy, but somtims you can here shooting at niht. I miss you. Im not alowd to get letres from Jamie so its nice to get yours. Ther is a big girl here calld Stella, she's 18 and she helps me with the shothand in the evneings bacuse shes got her diploma and she works in the ofice. Shes sort of second in comand to miss Scott and miss Cassidy who are the ladies in charge at helens hope. only we call them Scottie and Cassie & they know but they dont mind. five girls went home last week, theyre familys didnt want them in the city with the election coming up so the hostle is nice and quiet at the minit but Stella is woryed becas they need girls to sew in ther factory

I raelly miss you. write soon. I hope its not to boring without me.

Love
Catherine

PS dont tell Mammy about this, I dont want her worrying about me

PPS do you ever see Jamie about the town?

This was an epic for Catherine; I imagined her writing it, tongue poking out in concentration, hair on end because she ran her hands through it when she was frazzled. I was in the same class as her in the convent even though she was older, and I always helped her when she got muddled. My heart turned over at the idea of her struggling at this college on her own – how dare anyone rap her knuckles! Catherine had thin white hands with a few freckles which she tried to scrub away with lemon juice; they were great hands for kneading dough or icing buns, and the idea of someone deliberately hurting them made my throat ache. For the first time I wished I was in Belfast not for the adventure, not just to escape from home, but to help her. A bully called Ivy! I couldn't bear it. There had been a few bullies at the convent in Mullankeen, and I'd always dealt with them for Catherine. A girl called Noreen Boyle still crossed the street when she saw me, remembering the time I'd bloodied her nose for calling Catherine stupid. Daddy beat me – the only time he ever did – but it was worth it. (I think he beat me because Noreen Boyle's daddy was the solicitor in the town; if he'd been a farm labourer or a mill worker he wouldn't have minded so much.)

At tea that night I came right out with it.

'Poor Catherine's really unhappy up in Belfast,' I said. She hadn't asked me not to tell *my* family.

Daddy looked mildly interested; Leo didn't take his eyes off his plate.

'The teachers pick on her,' I went on, 'and someone in the hostel too. You know what she's like.'

'God love her,' Daddy said. 'She was always a gentle wee soul. But she's better off where she is. Away from – well, away from here.'

'But would you not like me to get away from here?' I asked. 'I was thinking, I could go to the college too and keep an eye on her.' I made my eyes wide and innocent and concerned. 'She's always had me to stick up for her. She can't manage on her own.'

'And what makes you think we can?' Daddy asked.

'Never mind sticking up for Catherine,' Leo said. 'Your place is to stay here and look after us.'

Daddy and Leo didn't agree about everything but at times like this it felt like they were ganged up against me, two grown men against a fifteen-year-old girl.

'And there's too much political unrest,' Daddy went on. 'Belfast isn't a good place to be. Personally I think your Auntie May overreacted, sending her there.'

'And Jamie McMahon's on the run,' Leo said. 'It's the talk of the country. Imagine if Catherine were still here – the danger –'

I didn't know how he knew what the talk of the country was, unless he talked to farmers when he was out on his endless walks, or to old rogues in Fox's.

'You mean he'd ask her to run away with him?' I could scarcely get the words out for the thrill of such a situation.

I imagined me and Catherine helping Jamie to escape, sprinting across dark fields at dead of night. Or, no, we'd have to keep to the shadow of the hedgerows. Even better! It would be so romantic. Catherine and Jamie would be

21

holding hands, anticipating the moment of parting when he reached safety, wherever that would be. But what would my role be, apart from comforting Catherine when, through my courage and ingenuity, we got Jamie safely away? I tried to place Flora in the scene too – after all, she hadn't wanted Jamie to be dismissed. Maybe she would give him Moonshine, her beloved pony, to escape on. Oh, yes! Because she would be broken-hearted at her noble sacrifice for the greater good of Ireland, and I would have to comfort her. I imagined her dark hair tickling my face as I hugged her.

But then I remembered that in real life Jamie might have been involved in shooting a policeman. And that Flora Galbraith was a Protestant who certainly wouldn't be helping an IRA man escape, let alone on her beloved pony. Maybe Jamie shouldn't actually escape – he could be shot, trying to ...

'Don't be silly, Polly.' Daddy's voice barged in to my dream. I blinked, as I often did when I came back from one of my wild imaginings, like a mole meeting the light. Sometimes I thought how lucky it was that you couldn't see other people's thoughts. People would think I was mad if they could see mine.

Or bad.

Leo was hunched over his plate, pushing his lamb chop around it. I wondered what his thoughts and imaginings were, but maybe it was just as well I didn't know. He had been drinking – I could smell it on his breath – and his face was reddened, his eyes bloodshot.

'It's time you grew up,' Daddy said, 'and learned a bit of sense.'

'I am being sensible. I'm suggesting I should learn some useful skills. I could help with the business,' I said. 'I could do the book-keeping, Daddy. You always say the accounts give you a headache.'

Leo gave a snort. 'You can barely count,' he said.

I glared at him. This was obviously one of those times when the drink made him nasty.

'I only couldn't do arithmetic at school because Sister Mary Agnes was a certified lunatic,' I said loftily.

'Don't speak ill of a woman of God,' Daddy said. 'And there's no question of you learning clerical skills. I do all that.'

'But you have to do everything since … I mean, now. I thought it would be a help.'

'If you'd like to help,' Daddy said, 'you can practise your sewing. I can always do with a hand for alterations.'

I let out a deep sigh. Sewing! I used to like sewing when I was a wee girl. I did it with Mammy, making clothes for teddies and embroidered needlecases and pillowslips. She encouraged me because she said it was my only ladylike accomplishment. After Mammy died, Daddy had given me an old carpet bag with some of her sewing things in: scissors, pincushion, a box of thread, a measuring tape rolled and neatly tied with a piece of pink ribbon. Some scraps of fabric left over from things she'd made for us all. I never opened the bag; I couldn't bear to remember Mammy sitting by the fire on winter nights, sewing by the lamplight. Nowadays I only did boring old darning and patching, and the thought of sewing made me feel like someone was pressing hard on a bruise inside me.

I changed the subject to show them I wasn't a child, but someone old enough and sensible enough to be sent to Belfast.

'So the election's next week,' I said. 'The first elections in Northern Ireland.'

Daddy made a snorting sound. 'It'll never last, this Northern Ireland nonsense. The unionists are calling it a Protestant state for Protestant people. Sure people round here'll never put up with that. Nationalists to a man, more or less. They'll have to put this bit of the country into the south and have done with it.'

'To a man?' I said. 'What about the women?'

Daddy made a dismissive gesture.

'The British don't give a damn,' Leo said. 'They think we're just inconvenient peasants. And the ones down in Dublin think the same.'

'What's changed your tune?' I demanded. 'You were keen enough on the British when you went to fight for them.'

'Aye, well, more fool me.'

'Yes, more fool you, but you're not the one has to put up with what everybody says about the town.' I'd never said this to Leo before – none of us ever talked about the fact that people didn't approve of him fighting for the British and that they took it out on the rest of us. Daddy never mentioned any trouble about the shop again, but he often had that stooped look about him these days and his mouth had grown tight, as if he was holding something in.

'Children!' Daddy said.

'He's not a child,' I said. 'He should be the one out scrubbing the walls of the shop, not you. You're an old man.'

'I'm fifty-one,' Daddy said.

'We're the ones that suffer because of Leo,' I went on. 'And you just let him carry on like a spoilt, drunk baby. I wish he'd never gone to the blasted war.'

'Polly!'

And then I said the thing that had been building up inside me since 1919, the thing I hardly ever let myself take out and look at, the thing that made me kick the sheets for weeks afterwards because it was so terrible.

The thing that changed my life.

'I wish he'd never come home. I wish he'd died instead of Mammy. He killed her anyway.'

The air round the table turned into needles. Leo sprang up, grabbed my hair at the nape of my neck and yanked it hard. My head jerked back and my eyes watered.

'You wee bitch,' he said.

He aimed a blow at my head. I squirmed away and as his fist hit one cheek, my other cheek bashed against the back of my chair. Pain exploded inside my head. My hands shot up to protect my face.

Daddy was shouting and Leo was shouting and I tried to scream at them to stop, but all that came out was a strangled whimper. And then I blacked out.

Chapter 4

THE kitchen was silent. The food sat congealing on the plates. A fly fed on my meat, pausing every so often to run its legs over its head. I couldn't touch my own head without wincing.

Daddy and Leo had gone. Leo had beaten me and Daddy had left me. I couldn't even start to think about which was worse. I forced myself to stand, head swimming, knees shuddering, and staggered upstairs to my bedroom, pausing often to lean on the wall of the staircase. I couldn't let myself form any actual thoughts or words; I was only putting one foot in front of the other.

In the glass in my bedroom I saw myself: one cheek red and swelling, the side of my head puffy above my right ear. But no blood. That would make things easier. I wouldn't have to wait and clean myself up.

I took Mammy's old sewing bag, and on top of the sewing things I squashed in a few frocks rolled up small, my comb and toothbrush and the least shabby of my undies and nighties – how strange that the draper's daughter should have such scruffy linen! I looked longingly at my shelf of school stories – it would be such a comfort to have some of them with me, but they were bulky and heavy and the bag was already bursting.

Then I went into Leo's room and took his money sock. I didn't know how much it would cost me to run away to Belfast, but there were several sovereigns and half-sovereigns. I felt no guilt. If I was indeed going to the bad, he had sent me on my way.

Chapter 5

THERE were so many people at Queen's Quay, pushing and jostling and shouting over my head, that I thought I'd arrived in the middle of one of the riots I'd heard about. I felt tiny and lost and scared, my aching head dizzy again with the tumult. But I soon realised that there wasn't anything going on; this was just the city. So many people, all different, some in posh clothes and fancy hats, some shabby and ragged, and I didn't know anybody, or their grannies or their cousins or their sisters. Nobody looked at me as if to say, *Isn't wee Polly McCabe awful bad/noisy/a disappointment to her daddy?* Nobody took the smallest bit of notice of me. And though it was scary, especially as I couldn't see Catherine anywhere – I had wired her my arrival time but I was hours late because the trains had been so messed about – it also made me feel free.

But where was Catherine? I hadn't doubted that she would meet me, but I had had no idea how busy and scary Belfast would be. I'd imagined somewhere like Newry or Dundalk or Armagh. For the first time I doubted my great plan. Why hadn't I just run next door to Auntie May?

She'd have comforted me. Or maybe not; maybe she'd have said I must have deserved it. Maybe she'd have asked me what I had done. What I had said.

'Polly?' A hand touched my sleeve and I jumped. 'Cath– oh.'

Not Catherine. A man, tall and red-haired. Leo's age or older. A stranger. I flinched and my hand flew up to my cheek.

'Catherine's over there.' He glanced over his shoulder and sure enough, there was Catherine, looking big-eyed and jittery, but reassuringly familiar.

'I couldn't let her come alone,' the man said. 'Not the way things are.'

I immediately felt stupid at having expected Catherine to meet me, but she ran forward and hugged me.

'Your face!' she said.

'Don't look at it.'

'How did –?'

'Don't ask.'

The man reached for my bag. 'I'm Sandy Reid,' he said. 'I help out at Helen's Hope.'

'Sandy's come to escort us.' Catherine sounded excited and proud, her face bright the way it was when Jamie McMahon had smiled at her at Mass. I hoped she hadn't lost her heart to this Mr Sandy Reid.

I'd much rather have been alone with Catherine. Maybe I'd have been able to tell her more about why I was here.

'Stay close,' Sandy said. 'The city's busy.'

We went outside, and soon I was glad of him, though a wee bit ashamed of myself for being so grateful for a male escort. The air smelt coally and thick after the soft clear air round Mullankeen. Huge buildings, some stone but mostly red brick, reared up on both sides of the street. A tram rattled past, and a couple of motor cars as well as carts. Everyone seemed to be in a great rush. Catherine tried to talk to me but the roar of people and traffic drowned out her words. I could only smile and hope I didn't look as nervous as I felt. I was meant to be the brave one. We crossed a bridge over a smelly brown river and down a long road on the other side. Warehouses and offices gave way to houses and shops. Posters were tied to most of the lamp posts with photos of men and slogans I didn't understand:

EX-SOLDIERS:
DON'T BETRAY YOUR COLLEAGUES
WHO SHED THEIR BLOOD!

and

VOTE FOR UNION, HOME AND EMPIRE.

British union flags, red, white and blue, hung from windows, even in ordinary houses. I shivered. For the first time I understood why both Catherine and Flora had been anxious about coming to the city. It was another country. I couldn't imagine Flora Galbraith here. We turned down a long road lined with shops. Streets of terraced houses ran off it, the doors opening right on to the pavements.

'Sandy! Catherine!' Pounding footsteps, and a tall, fair girl of about eighteen was standing beside us. She nodded at me. I could see her noticing my bruised face and trying not to show any reaction. 'And you must be Polly? You made it safely. Good for you. Was it a horrible journey? I'm Stella, from Helen's Hope.'

'I had to change a few times,' I said. I remembered the name Stella from Catherine's letters. 'The timetables were all disrupted.' I tried to sound nonchalant, as if I caught trains all the time, as if I hadn't spent the journey in constant fear of getting in the wrong train, of needing the lavatory, of waking from fitful headachy dozes to find Leo looming above me, fist clenched. Something about this tall, breezy girl made me want to impress her.

'Everything's disrupted,' Sandy said. He looked Stella up and down. 'Including you! Looks like you've escaped from a madhouse. I thought Labour rallies were peaceful.'

Stella let out a long breath. She was hatless, her bobbed fair hair in a tangle, her face scraped and her skirt torn, but even so there was something splendid about her. Something free and daring. 'It was nasty,' she said.

'What happened?' Sandy asked.

Stella's face hardened. 'It was a peaceful election meeting at the Ulster Hall,' she said. 'And those bloody – sorry, but those bloody loyalists hijacked it. They just marched in and took over, turned it into their own meeting.'

'They don't like Labour,' Sandy said. 'They think they're communists. They call them the Red Faction.'

'They don't like anyone who stands for internationalism and looking forwards and outwards. They hate the fact that there are three Socialists standing in Belfast. They want to keep it tribal.' Stella shook back her messy hair and grinned. 'I bashed some of them with my elbows,' she said. 'That's the only language they understand.'

'Stella!' Sandy said. 'One of these days you'll get hurt.'

'Don't worry, Polly, Helen's Hope is very safe,' Catherine said.

'We'll cut down by the Short Strand,' Stella said. 'Polly looks exhausted and it's quicker.'

'I don't know,' Sandy said. 'Ever since the Catholic church was targeted last year –'

'It's too early for trouble,' Stella said.

But she was wrong. We turned down a street which even I could see was different. Same small red-brick houses. Different posters, republican flags like the ones I'd been noticing about Mullankeen recently. I felt myself relax.

But not for long.

'Damn,' Sandy said. 'Look.'

Ahead of us, where the street met what looked like a main road, some youths hung round the bottom of a lamp-post. Another boy was up the lamp-post attaching a union flag to the top. He gave a yell of triumph and his mates cheered. Catherine's hand crept into mine, the way it used to do when Noreen Boyle bullied her.

Stella broke away from us and started to march towards the youths. 'Hey,' she said. 'You might want to think about where you're putting your flags.'

'Stella!' Sandy sounded uneasy. 'It's not worth it. Maybe we should turn back.'

He glanced back the way we'd come and swore under his breath.

Another crowd of boys was advancing from behind, some of them carrying metal bin lids. They must have been told about the flag and had come out to protest.

Stella marched on, her shoulders back and her chin in the air. Even though I was scared I couldn't help admiring her; she was like an Amazon warrior. Sandy lengthened his stride so he was beside her, and I scuttled to keep up.

They might have been only boys but they looked and sounded nasty.

'Come out of your holes, you fenian scum,' shouted one.

Behind us the local lads yelled back. 'Get back to your own streets, you orange bastards and take your bloody British flag with you.'

'Ulster's British!' shouted the boy up the lamp-post. He shimmied down lightly and stood on the footpath, his arms folded over his chest. The boys spread across the street.

Stella snorted. 'Let us past,' she called. 'This is a public highway. You've no right to stop us.'

I don't suppose the boys knew who we were; they were just lads looking for trouble and we had walked into it. Caught in the middle.

'What are yous?' shouted one of the boys.

'People,' Stella said.

Of course I knew they meant *Are you Catholics or Protestants?* I could see how much that mattered here. In Mullankeen it mattered too: we had our own churches and schools and the Protestants – like Flora Galbraith – mostly lived in the bigger houses, but nobody stood in the street and yelled at you. Or banged bin lids which the boys behind us had started to do. The ground shuddered under my feet. Suddenly I was furious rather than afraid, the black bud inside me reaching out to meet the anger of the boys and their stupid bin lids. I wanted to say something magical that would make the boys let us through and reassure Catherine that I was still her protector, even if I had turned up looking black and blue, like a victim. I hated thinking about Leo, but maybe Leo could help me now.

'My brother was in the British army,' I shouted. 'He fought for that flag.' Surely that would impress them? I remembered the posters I'd seen. VOTE FOR UNION, HOME AND EMPIRE. 'He fought for Union, Home and Empire!' I yelled. The words felt strange in my mouth, as strange as summoning Leo – my enemy now – to my defence.

I'd forgotten the other boys. The ones closing in behind us. The ones who hated the very idea of the British army. And the flag. 'Get them!' one yelled, and a stone whizzed past my head.

'Polly!' Catherine said. 'What a stupid –'

We would have to run. But we were caught between two seething crowds. All we could do was push through and hope. Sandy was big and strong and Stella and I were fuelled by rage, and Catherine – well, Catherine was whimpering with fear, her hand digging into mine so hard it hurt.

But the stones and bits of brick kept coming. And then there was a cry, and Stella crumpled to the ground in front of me. Blood spread into the gutter. The boys melted away.

Sandy knelt down beside her and lifted her in his arms.

'She's dead!' I cried. This was what my big mouth had done.

Chapter 6

SUDDENLY the street was empty, the flag hanging limply from the post.

I knelt beside Sandy and Stella. Sandy was shaking; Stella was horribly still. Blood ran into the gutter. A fragment of orangey-red brick lay beside Stella. It looked innocent. It was more innocent than I was. I might not have thrown the brick but I was the reason it had been thrown.

The bad didn't seem such a glamorous place to be if it meant people getting hurt.

'She's not dead,' Catherine whispered. 'She can't be.'

'No – look,' Sandy said.

Stella's eyes flickered. Relief flooded me.

'We need to get her away from here.' Sandy picked her up as if she was a child or an injured dog. Her fair hair, matted with blood, lay in strands over his arm. He looked down at her white bleeding face and muttered, 'You'll be all right.'

'No, she won't,' I said, relief making me bold. 'She needs a doctor.' Stella came round more and moaned and looked whiter than ever against the grey tweed of Sandy's jacket.

'I have to get to the rally,' she murmured. 'I don't want to be late.'

'Shh,' Sandy said. 'Don't worry.' He stroked a bloody lock of her hair very gently off her face.

'D'you think he's in love with her?' Catherine whispered in my ear.

'Never mind that,' I said. 'Is it far?' I asked loudly. I picked up my bag.

'About half a mile,' Sandy said.

It was the longest half-mile of my life. A tram rattled past us on the main road, and when it had passed we crossed over. Every so often Sandy staggered and gritted his teeth. Once he stopped and leaned against the gable end of a house, breathing hard. I could smell his sweat. His face wasn't white now; it was red with effort. Stella must be heavy; she was slim but tall.

'Are we nearly there?' I asked.

The streets running off the main road all looked the same – long rows of red-brick terraced houses. I didn't see how any of them could be a home for girls.

'Yes.' Sandy's voice was low and strained. 'Next street. Number 45.' In a different voice, to Stella, he said, 'Not far. You're going to be all right.'

I wasn't so sure about that; Stella was whiter than anyone I'd ever seen. As bad as Mammy the night she died. She'd been nursing Leo, who had come home from France coughing and sweating with the flu, and when she'd got sick herself she wouldn't rest, and then she'd just fallen down dead. She hadn't looked as bad as Stella did now.

'Should Catherine and I run ahead?' I suggested. 'Let them know?'

He nodded. 'Tell them to get Dr Scott,' he said.

Catherine and I flew down the darkening street. After a short row of terraced houses, the street broke up into bigger houses, semi-detached and then a few detached. Number 45 was the very last one. Its bright yellow front door glowed through the dusk. I flung myself up the steps and banged hard on the shining brass knocker. For ages nobody came, and I stood gasping for breath, longing to rest on the yellow-painted summer seat under the front bay window. Finally a light shone in the porch, and the door was pulled open by a woman with short brown hair and spectacles.

'It's Stella, Miss Cassidy,' Catherine said at once. 'She's been hurt – Sandy's carrying her home. He says get the doctor.'

Miss Cassidy's eyes widened. 'Oh! I knew this would happen!' She turned and called down the hall, 'Alice! Phone your brother! Stella's been hurt. Tell him to come at once.'

I guessed Alice must be the sister of the Dr Scott Sandy had mentioned. Which would make her Miss Scott. Scottie, I remembered Catherine calling her.

I heard an exclamation from inside the house and then what must have been someone lifting a telephone and speaking into it. And then Sandy was at the bottom of the steps with Stella in his arms. Miss Cassidy – Cassie, I remembered from Catherine's letter – held the door wide and said, 'Back parlour, Sandy. Lay her on the couch.'

Nobody took any notice of me and Catherine but we followed them through the long, darkish hall to a sitting room. I wondered where all the girls were – in bed? I shrank back into the bay of the window and watched them all. It was like watching a moving picture I'd missed the start of, guessing who everyone was and what their part in the story was. Except I wasn't just watching – I'd played a part. Stella had been hit by that brick because of me and my big mouth. If they knew that, surely they'd throw me out in the street? After all, I didn't know for sure that they wanted me in the first place. I hadn't really given them much choice.

Catherine and I just stood in the corner and watched what was happening. Gently, Sandy laid Stella down on a couch and Cassie bent over her. Another woman joined them. ('That's Scottie,' Catherine whispered.) 'He's on his way,' she said. 'Sandy, sit down before you fall down.' Scottie took Sandy by the shoulder and manoeuvred him into an armchair. Only then did I notice he was clutching one of his arms and that his face was crumpled in pain.

'You're hurt too,' Scottie said.

'This stupid arm,' he said through gritted teeth.

Cassie dabbed at the blood on Stella's face with a clean handkerchief. 'I think the blood's slowing.'

'What happened?' Scottie asked. 'Have we any brandy?'

'She's unconscious!' said Cassie. She was about forty, with a school-marmish look – short hair and glasses and clothes that could only be called sensible.

'Not for Stella, you donkey!' said Scottie. I'd have been cross at being called a donkey but Cassie smiled. 'Sandy looks like he's going to keel over.'

'I'm fine,' he said but he obviously wasn't. He was grey and shaking, cradling his hurt arm, sweat standing out on his forehead.

Scottie left the room and came back shortly with a glass of brandy which she handed to Sandy. 'Drink it,' she said. 'It'll revive you a bit.'

He obeyed, and sure enough he started to look better. He set the glass down on the table by his armchair. 'Stella's the one you should be worrying about. Where's the doctor?'

'On his way,' Scottie said. 'What actually happened? I heard there was trouble at the rally.'

'No, she was hit by a brick in the street. There were some lads having a stand-off and – och, you know what she's like.' He shuddered. He didn't say anything about my part in it.

Cassie turned to me. 'And you must be Polly? I'm sorry you've had such a violent introduction to Belfast. Catherine here was very insistent that we find room for you. She says you're just the kind of girl for Helen's Hope.'

Catherine blushed. I couldn't imagine her being brave enough to be insistent. I felt a little flutter of affection for her.

'It's an unorthodox way of arriving,' Cassie went on, 'but we can talk about that in the morning. Obviously I'll have to talk to your father.' She looked closely at my face. 'Maybe I should ask the doctor to look at that face of yours.'

I bit my lip. 'It's fine,' I said. 'I hardly feel it.'

'The best thing for you girls is bed,' Scottie said. 'Polly, I've put you in the Lavender Room with Catherine.'

Lavender Room! Like a school story.

A bell rang out and Scottie jumped up. 'That'll be Eddie.'

Eddie was obviously Dr Scott; he came in with his black leather bag and went straight to Stella. 'Basin of water, please,' he said, and Scottie scuttled out.

He took out a stethoscope and listened to Stella's heartbeat. We all watched in silence. I minded desperately that she should be all right. I felt so guilty. The doctor opened and closed Stella's eyelids. Scottie came back with the basin of warm water and he washed the blood from her face. Then he took scissors from his bag and cut away the hair around the wound on her temple. His hands were gentle and deft. I found myself watching with a kind of awe as he took out some white gauze and bandaged Stella's head. It must be great to have hands so skilled. Scottie handed him things as he needed them. The whole room was holding its breath. Dr Scott was a man of few words and the only sounds were the snip of his scissors and then a tinny clink as he placed them into the bowl of water.

He turned to us. 'She'll be fine,' he said and the room relaxed. 'She should come round shortly. I'm afraid you'll need to check on her every couple of hours during the night, just in case.'

'Of course,' Scottie said.

'Send for me if you've any concerns – if she starts to vomit or seems very disorientated – but it should just be a matter of sleeping it off. Can you help me get her up to bed?' He lifted Stella up and, accompanied by Scottie, left the room.

When they had gone, Sandy frowned at the carpet. 'I should have stopped her –'

'It wasn't your fault, Sandy,' Cassie said. 'We all know how impetuous she is. She rushes in where angels fear to tread.'

I waited for him to say it hadn't been that simple, that I had said something stupid which had provoked the boys to throw stones and bricks. But he didn't. Did he not remember? Had he not heard? I knew I should confess. But what if they decided to send me away? After all, I'd invited myself here in the first place. For once, I couldn't make myself say a word, and then the doctor came back.

'Eddie,' Cassie said, 'Sandy's strained his arm. He carried Stella all the way here.'

Sandy looked embarrassed. 'Old war wound,' he explained. 'God, I sound about ninety.'

Dr Scott went to Sandy, flexed his arm and said it would take time and rest. 'When did you hurt it?'

'1918. Kemmel Ridge.'

'Looks like you were lucky not to lose it,' Dr Scott said. 'It's definitely not made for heroics.' Their war-talk created their own little man's world in this very female place. Leo never talked about the war. Not one word. *Ugh* – I wasn't going to think about Leo. You couldn't compare him to Sandy, who'd obviously not come back without a scratch. 'This will help with the pain.' The doctor rooted

42

in his bag and handed Sandy a small bottle. 'Take two now. One later if you can't sleep.'

'Thanks.' Sandy took the bottle with his good hand, but couldn't unscrew it one-handed. Dr Scott took it back, opened it, and in silence handed Sandy a couple of pills. He washed them down with the dregs of the brandy.

'Go home now, Sandy,' Cassie said. 'Eddie can drive you. We have enough problems without having a man here late in the evening. Even a respectable employee like you.' Sandy smiled faintly. 'And don't come in tomorrow,' Cassie said. 'The garden will be fine.'

When they had gone, Cassie said, 'He will come. He can't keep away, bless him.' I wondered if that was because of Stella. Was Catherine right that he was in love with her? There seemed to be a lot going on in this place that I didn't understand. Cassie smiled at me. 'Don't look so worried, girls. Stella's tough. She'll wake up none the worse.'

I remembered what I'd said, how stupid I'd been, what I'd made happen. I didn't think Helen's Hope would want to keep me then. Catherine squeezed my hand, but I didn't feel like squeezing back.

Chapter 7

THE Lavender Room wasn't much like a school story dorm. It smelt of sweat and I had to clamber and squeeze to get to my bed in the corner. I counted three other beds. Two had bright patchwork quilts on them – I recognised Catherine's blue and yellow one – and two, including mine, had only plain grey blankets.

'No chatting,' Cassie said. 'It's late and Polly's had a difficult journey.' She didn't mention what had happened in the street.

She might as well have told us not to breathe. The minute she left the two girls sat up in bed.

'Where did you come from?' said the girl without a quilt. She had flinty eyes and an accent like gravel, like the boys in the street.

'Mullankeen.'

She wrinkled her nose. She was about my age, mousey-haired, with a thin plait. 'That stupid place where Catherine comes from? She doesn't seem to know where it is.'

I narrowed my eyes at her. 'Are you Ivy?' I asked.

'How d'you know?'

I raised my eyebrows in what I hoped was an enigmatic way. I wasn't going to let on what Catherine had said about Ivy in her letters, but if she thought she was going to get away with bullying her she'd have me to answer to.

Catherine rushed in. 'Yes, that's Ivy and the other girl is Tessa. She's new. We're pals.'

Pals? So Catherine wasn't all alone, desperate for me? Tessa had a tumble of black curls and sparkling eyes like a smart puppy's. She grinned, showing small white teeth. I smiled back, a little uncertainly, and tried to take off my frock and put my nightie on without showing too much underwear. Then I got into bed. It was a small iron bed, the sheets worn but fresh.

'I suppose you're a fenian like your cousin,' Ivy said in a resigned voice.

'Ivy!' Tessa sounded shocked. 'We're not meant to ask.'

'We can ask,' Ivy said. 'We're just not meant to mind.'

'Oh, for goodness' sake, who cares?' Tessa said. 'Sure we're all just one happy family here at Helen's Hope. Living together, working together, learning together,' she said in a singsong voice. 'You know what Stella says.'

I tried not to think about Stella being hurt. 'Catherine's told me a bit about Helen's Hope,' I said, 'but not exactly what it is.'

'Depends who you ask,' Tessa said. 'My ma thinks it's respectable lodgings to keep us away from bad boys.' She grinned and Catherine blushed.

I hoped she hadn't told anyone about Jamie McMahon. She seemed very thick with this Tessa.

'Cassie thinks it's a place to drum some learning into us. She used to be a teacher – you can tell by the look of her, can't you?' Ivy said.

'Stella thinks it's an experiment in modern living and is going to change the world.' Tessa rolled her eyes and giggled.

I didn't like them making fun of Stella – when junior girls in the stories criticised the head girl they always turned out to be the baddies. I didn't want to throw my lot in with baddies before I found out what the other girls were like. One thing to go to the bad myself, another to be dragged there by girls I wasn't sure about.

'Reverend Hamill from the Presbyterian church thinks it's a den of iniquity full of girls who are no better than they should be,' Tessa went on.

'And God knows what the Catholic priest thinks,' Catherine joined in for the first time.

'Who cares!' Ivy said.

'Och, it's not bad,' Tessa said. 'They go on a lot about tolerance and understanding.'

'So is it like school?'

'Not really,' Tessa said. 'Cassie makes you go to classes if you can't read and write well.' Catherine looked sheepish and Ivy smirked. 'There's a sewing factory for girls to learn a trade. And make a bit of money.'

'That's where you could work, Poll,' Catherine said eagerly.

Tessa went on, 'But some of us just go out to work and lodge here. I'm at a lemonade factory.' She sighed. 'It's awful boring.' Then she perked up. 'I don't like putting labels on lemonade bottles, and I hate the troubles in

the city, but I love the picture houses and the music hall.'
She started to sing, 'The boy I love is up in the gallery.'

I couldn't help giggling. 'Are you allowed to go to music halls and picture houses and cafés?' I asked.

Tessa stopped singing. 'Not exactly. But a girl can hope. They don't lock us up.'

Ivy pursed her lips. 'You'd need locked up,' she said. 'Poor Sandy hides when he sees you.'

'Sandy isn't interested in *me*,' Tessa said sadly.

'I should think not.'

'He's too old for us,' Catherine said.

'Anyway, we all know who he's sweet on,' Tessa said.

Stella, I thought.

'Poor Stella got bashed on the head at the rally,' Tessa went on. 'I saw Dr Scott carrying her up the stairs. We all have to be quiet.'

'She has no place going to Labour rallies,' Ivy said. 'Asking for trouble. Mixing with commies.'

'It wasn't the rally,' Catherine said. 'It was some boys in the street.'

'How do you know?' Ivy demanded.

'We were there. Sandy was too.'

'I bet it was fenians hit her,' Ivy said.

'Girls!' A stern voice came from outside the room. 'No talking!'

'Flip sake,' Tessa muttered. 'It's like school.'

I only wished it was. I tried to settle down to sleep. The bed was comfortable and my body ached from tiredness, Leo's attack and the journey, but it was a long time before I slept, listening to the unfamiliar shufflings and huffings of the others, worrying about Daddy being lonely, worrying about Stella, and about the morning, and whether I would be allowed to stay here. Or if I really wanted to. So far, neither Belfast nor Helen's Hope were exactly what I'd been hoping for.

Chapter 8

NEXT morning was all bustle: girls racing off to factories and mills, girls grumbling their way to offices and shops. I felt shy and lost in the dining room, surrounded by all the chatter. Cassie stood up after breakfast to wish everyone a good day and to warn them to be careful.

'You know how troubled the streets are at the moment,' she said. 'And some of you may know how close that came yesterday when our own dear Stella was hurt in a ... an *incident*.' There was a buzz of concern and excitement. 'She'll be fine,' she said, 'but she's to stay quietly in bed. She won't be in her office for a few days, nor able to help with classes until further notice' – a few girls perked up – 'but you'll be pleased to know that you won't miss out. Edith will hear your reading and Miss Scott will help with mathematics. So nobody need lose out.' They drooped. 'Sewing girls – Brigid tells me you did sterling work last week to get the banner finished. Well done.'

'Polly,' she said, as she passed me on her way to the door, 'you and I need to have a chat. Come with me.'

Cassie's study was a small, neat room on the first floor. Books lined the walls and the large desk was piled with papers. I sat in the chair she beckoned me to, and waited.

'Now, Polly,' she said. 'You've come to us in a very unorthodox way.'

'I know.'

'I've spoken to your father on the telephone. He was very shocked at your running away. You caused him great worry.'

But he went out and left me! Leo beat me till I fainted and Daddy just left the room! He can't have been that worried. The words jabbed at my brain but I just hung my head and looked sorry. I wondered how much she knew.

'But he is willing for you to stay here for the time being. Until things settle down at home.' I wondered if this referred to Leo or to the trouble in Mullankeen, but I didn't want to ask. 'I can see that you have been subjected to some violence.' She did that thing of trying not to look at my face. 'I appreciate that you must have been driven to desperate measures.'

'Yes.' But the sympathy in her voice made me uncomfortable. I didn't want to be seen as a victim. 'But I've wanted to come for ages. When my brother hit me, it – well, it gave me an excuse, I suppose.'

She looked surprised. 'I see. And what made you want to come to Helen's Hope so badly?'

'It sounded fun,' I said. 'Like boarding school.'

Cassie waited, obviously expecting something better, so I rushed on with what I hoped was a more noble motivation. 'I missed Catherine.' I didn't want to tell tales so I didn't go into detail about Ivy picking on her. 'I've always looked after her.'

'I see. And what can you contribute to Helen's Hope? If we let you stay.'

I gulped. 'Contribute?'

'Yes, Polly, this is a community. A community which, I don't mind telling you, exists under some pressure. Especially at the moment. Tensions in the city are high and yesterday – well, you saw how close it got. Some people are very suspicious of us – people who don't approve of what we stand for – tolerance and acceptance. People who can't understand women living together without men. I can't accept any girl who might jeopardise our reputation in the city, such as it is. We want Helen's Hope to be a safe haven for young women. A beacon of hope in uncertain times. So far all I know of you is that you are – shall we say impetuous? I need to know I can trust you to be steady and reliable.'

She sounded exactly like the headmistresses in the books apart from all the stuff about violence and politics.

'I'll be good,' I promised.

'It's not just about being good. And it's certainly not about fun, though obviously we want you to be happy. Every girl contributes something. Those who can pay for their board do so. I understand your father is happy to –'

I blushed. 'Of course he is,' I said. 'I'm not a charity case!'

'There is no suggestion of charity at Helen's Hope. Please understand that. No difference is made between the girls who can contribute financially and those who cannot. Can you read and write?' she went on. 'Your cousin struggles –'

51

'I can read and write the best,' I said, stung that she might think otherwise. 'I love reading. And I can clean and scrub and make beds and all the skivvy work. I've been keeping house since … for ages.' I didn't want to talk about Mammy dying. 'I could do the housework. I noticed your skirting boards were very dusty. You could do with a better maid.'

'We have no maid. We all take turns with the housework,' Cassie said drily. 'Some girls are more skilled in the housewifely arts than others.'

'And I can sew. Catherine said you needed more people in the sewing factory?'

'We did, though things have been very quiet lately. But I daresay we could make use of you. It's only a cottage industry – we've converted the outhouses into the factory – but it pays for itself. Or it's meant to.' Her face clouded. 'It's not always easy to get orders.'

'I'm good at sewing.'

'Well, Brigid can see how you shape up this morning. She's in charge. But, Polly, you're very much on trial. If we have any doubts about your influence … We need to be able to trust our girls, more than ever in these times. Can I trust you?'

'Yes,' I said. And I really, really meant it.

Chapter 9

THE sewing factory, at the far end of the stone-flagged yard, was an ordinary shed except for three big glass windows set into the roof. Brigid, a tall girl of about twenty, with dark plaits pinned round her head, met me at the door.

'Cassie tells me you're an experienced seamstress,' she said.

For once I didn't feel at a disadvantage in this strange new world. And for the first time since Mammy died I felt that I wanted to sew, that it might make me feel closer to her.

'Yes.'

'It's curtains and nightshirts today.' Brigid felt along the wall, hit a switch and the room brightened almost at once. Six benches were lined up in two rows with something humped and big on top of each, covered in old white sheets. A big table at the top held rolls of fabric of all colours. Four girls filed in past us, took down overalls from hooks on the wall and took their seats without being asked. Ivy was there: she buttoned her overall with great care and heavy mouth-breathing and then took her place at her bench. She pulled off the white sheet from the humped

53

thing on the bench and I realised it was a sewing machine. A machine!

As soon as Ivy started sewing she seemed transformed. Her fingers were swift and sure as she pulled the fabric through and turned the wheel, while her foot trundled the pedal under her bench in a steady confident rhythm. The other girls were doing the same. Some of them were sewing something small and white, and the others had lengths of floral curtain fabric. There was a low buzz of chatter and the occasional giggle, but their wheels and feet and hands never stopped. The faster their wheels spun the deeper grew my despondency.

There was an empty bench near the far wall. 'There you go,' Brigid said, leading the way through the factory. She grabbed a striped overall and handed it to me and I put it on obediently. 'I'll keep an eye on you.'

I stared at the machines, at the girls whirring their wheels and trundling their feet as if it was the easiest thing in the world.

'Um,' I said, my fingers trembling as I tried to button the overall.

'What are you waiting for?'

I fastened the last button. 'I've never used a machine,' I said. 'It's hand sewing I can do.'

'Hand sewing?' Brigid looked at me as if I'd walked out of the last century.

'There was a machine at our shop,' I said, 'but I never learned to use it. I only sewed for – well, for fun. When Cassie said sewing, I thought –'

'You imagined a room full of pretty maids all sewing a fine seam by hand? Producing one dainty handkerchief a week maybe?'

'I didn't really know.' I supposed I had imagined myself sewing something exquisite and beautiful.

Brigid rolled her eyes. 'Ivy – get on with your work and stop staring.' She sighed. 'Right, well, I'll have to show you.'

'I'm sure I can pick it up,' I said. If Ivy could master it, so could I.

An hour later I wasn't so confident. In my mind I could do it. In my mind my hands and feet moved together and the wheel trundled and the needle went up and down steadily and my seams were straight and true. In real life my hands juddered and stuttered and the needle stopped and started and the fabric – an old piece of cambric Brigid said would do for practising on – was puckered and grubby and damp with my tears of frustration. I'd lost count of how many times Brigid had cried out, 'Watch your finger!' as I got too close to the relentless needle. Once I leaned over too far and the needle caught my front hair and I screamed; I thought I was being scalped, and my whole head and face were still tender from Leo's attack.

'Calm down, you eejit,' Brigid said. 'I told you to put your hair back tight.'

'I tried to,' I said, rubbing my forehead, 'but it's so frizzy, bits jump out.'

'You'll have to wear a cap.' Brigid's own hair was smooth, not a single hair escaping. She raised her voice. 'Can someone see if there's a spare cap?'

A round-faced girl with brown hair shingled close to her head and steel-rimmed spectacles came up with a white cotton cap and I pulled it on. It felt tight and strange.

The girl grinned at me. 'You should get shingled like me,' she said, and ran her hands over her neat head. She gestured towards the machine. 'It gets easier,' she said. 'And' – she lowered her voice – 'Brigid's nice really.'

'Thanks, Maggie, back to work,' Brigid said.

Every so often girls would come up to Brigid to ask her something, and occasionally she would have to go down to their machines to sort something out, but most of the time she was focused on me and my incompetence. Her own hands were quick and clever, and she had a small diamond ring on the left one, which told me she was engaged. She saw me looking at it and curled her hand so I couldn't see it.

'I don't know why you can't manage,' she said, sounding genuinely puzzled rather than mean. 'Everyone else can.'

'I'm stupid.' I'd never felt stupid before. It was badness I was always accused of. Stupidity felt much worse. At least badness had a dash to it. I'd always felt sorry for Catherine, and rushed to protect her when people teased her for being clumsy and slow, but for the first time I knew how it felt.

At half past ten Brigid rang a small hand bell and everyone stopped. I hadn't realised how loud the whirr of the machines was until they fell silent. My ears rang with the quiet. The girls stretched and rotated their shoulders and made their way to the door.

'Fifteen minutes!' Brigid shouted. 'And don't be coming back in here with sticky fingers!' To me she said, 'A cup of tea will help you.'

Scottie was in the kitchen with a big teapot and a pile of buns. Everyone took a bun and a mug of tea and drifted back outside. It was a lovely day. I followed them, too shy to speak to anyone. I bit into my bun which was a bit dry compared to the ones Catherine made at home. I pulled off my cap and scratched my damp, itchy hair.

'Polly? How are you getting on?'

I spun round to see Cassie and I immediately stopped scratching. I wanted to be able to say I'd had a great morning, but to my annoyance the tears that had been near the surface since my first abortive attempt to thread the bobbin spilled over. I tried to dash them away but she noticed.

'Oh, well,' she said. 'It takes practice.'

'But the machines are horrible. I keep thinking I'm going to cut my finger off. Or gouge a hole in it. And it's so noisy. My head's splitting.' I had a kick of homesickness, for standing at the back door, looking out at the green and purple hills behind us, the soft damp air misting my cheeks. In Belfast, even in the garden at Helen's Hope, the air felt gritty, and when I blew my nose my snatters were streaked with black. The dry crumbs of the bun scratched my throat. I gripped my white china mug tighter and muttered, 'I didn't think it'd be so hard.'

I hadn't noticed that Ivy and a girl I didn't know were standing behind us, but now Ivy let out a snort. 'Have you come up the Lagan in a bubble?' she demanded. I gawped. 'I mean, are you daft?' she went on. 'Have you ever been in a real factory?'

I shook my head dumbly.

'Leave her alone, Ivy,' her friend said, but Ivy pressed on. 'A hundred times as big,' she said. 'A thousand times as noisy. And the damp and the dust.' She held out her left hand and I saw with a sick jolt that the top of her wee finger was missing. 'I caught that on a loom when I was thirteen,' she said. 'My ma died of TB from years in the linen mills, coughing her lungs up every morning. This' – she gestured back at the low brick factory building, whose door was open to the sunny morning – 'is like a pretend factory. You don't know you're born.'

'Ivy,' Cassie said, 'that's not in the spirit of Hope House, is it? Don't let me catch you speaking like that again.' Before Ivy could react, the little hand bell rang out again and there was a lot of good-natured groaning and shuffling. Ivy's friend returned both their cups, and Ivy stalked back to the factory, her back very straight.

Maggie waited for me. 'Don't worry,' she said. 'Ivy's always a bit sharp. But she's right – the conditions here are far better than in normal factories. So try not to whinge – in a few days it'll come as easy to you as swimming to a duck.'

Maybe it was the cup of tea, or Maggie's kindness, or the warning of Ivy's missing fingertip, but after break I wasn't quite as stupid. Sometimes my fingers did what I wanted for whole seconds at a time, though the moment I stopped to think about what I was doing my foot would judder to a halt or even fall off the pedal. By the afternoon Brigid was leaving me for ten or twenty minutes to get on with her own work – she had to check every single item to make sure it was good enough, and she had to monitor the speed of production.

I was so focused on my puckered little squares of cambric that I hadn't noticed what the other girls were making, but at half past three, when we had an afternoon break, I looked at the basket beside Maggie's machine and saw that it was full of little nightshirts. She pulled one out to show me.

'Isn't it sweet?' she said.

It was very neatly made, in the softest blue-and-white striped cotton.

'I'll never be able to sew like that,' I said.

Ivy leaned over and said, 'They're for the poor wee bastards in St Something-or-Other's.'

'Ivy!' Brigid said and Ivy shrugged.

'That's what they are,' she said. 'Wee fenian bastards with no daddies.'

'Well, you've no call to use either of those words.' Brigid turned to me. 'We're making these for an orphanage in the west of the city. Cassie has a friend on the board of governors.'

'So it's for charity?' I asked.

'No, we get paid. The profits are added to the communal good and we get a small wage.'

'Just as well,' said Maggie. 'We're barely breaking even.'

'I think our fortune's going to change.' Ivy smiled a secret, satisfied smile.

Brigid moved in quickly. 'We'll be fine. Stella's typed up some adverts for the newspapers. They're sitting on her desk.' She gestured towards a door in the wall which led to what I guessed must be Stella's office. 'I'll take them to the newspaper offices this afternoon. Now get on, girls, and don't be gossiping.'

'My ma's always saying I'd be better off in a proper factory.' Maggie pushed her glasses up her nose.

'So why don't you go to one?' Ivy asked.

'Because I believe in Helen's Hope.'

Ivy rolled her eyes, but Maggie looked serious. She moved closer to me and said, 'I was a half-time doffer in a mill from I was ten. I wanted to stay at school, but we needed my pay. Only I took the whooping cough awful bad and then the scarlet fever and I wasn't fit to work. Here I can earn and learn and get my keep. Stella's teaching me book-keeping and typing. I'd love to work in an office and make something of myself. What I'd really love would be to go to commercial college.' She sighed and then brightened. 'But I manage all right with Stella helping.'

I thought of Catherine who had drooped off to college that morning, clearly dreading it, and once again I thought that the world was ill-divid. Though maybe Helen's Hope was trying to make it less so.

Brigid clapped her hands. 'Right,' she said. 'We're well up to speed with this order. Might as well start pressing what we have.' She looked round and all the girls began to stitch furiously. She sighed and said, 'Come on, just a couple of you.'

I whispered to Maggie, 'What does she want?'

'The things have to be pressed before they're packed. Nobody likes ironing.'

I shot my hand up. 'Brigid, I don't mind ironing.' I was used to ironing men's shirts, with their thick seams and long tails and awkward cuffs; these little nightshirts would be easy.

'Do you iron as well as you sew?'

I felt my cheeks burn but I was braver now. 'Even better,' I said, and Brigid laughed, but not unkindly.

'Oh, all right.'

'I'll help,' Maggie said.

The pressing took place in a wee outhouse beside the factory. After ten minutes it was boiling and I understood why pressing wasn't popular. Maggie pushed her hair off her face and rubbed her spectacles on her overall. I wedged the door open with a stone from the yard. I could see Sandy up a ladder against the main house, pulling leaves out of the gutters and collecting them in a bucket tied to his ladder. So he had ignored Cassie's advice to stay at home. It was funny how Sandy was quite posh but he did the dirty jobs. Maybe everyone at Helen's Hope was sort of playing – though the work and the dirt were real enough, whatever Ivy said about a pretend factory.

'At least it's quieter out here,' I said.

'You get used to the noise,' Maggie said, 'Sometimes it's as noisy in there as it is in our house with the whole six of us and Mam and Dad. I can't wait to take my commercial exams and get a job in an office. As long as I don't have to leave here; I don't want to go home.'

I didn't want to start talking about home and families.

'Maggie,' I asked. 'What did Ivy mean about the factory's fortunes changing?'

Maggie lowered her voice. 'I don't know,' she said. 'I have an idea but – I'm probably wrong. I hope I'm wrong.' Her voice changed. 'Watch out!' she said. 'You're singeing that nightshirt!'

Chapter 10

IT wasn't exactly like a duck learning to swim, but by the following day I was promoted to sewing real things instead of scraps.

'Curtains today – for Ellis House,' Brigid announced. 'Polly, I'm going to trust you to have a go. Just take your time and call me if you get into trouble, but it's just long straight seams.'

I was pleased to be trusted, but something nudged at my brain. Ellis House? Surely I'd heard that name before.

I whispered to Maggie, 'What's Ellis House?'

'It's a school,' Maggie said. 'A girls' school. Beside the park.'

So I was sewing curtains for Flora Galbraith's dormitory window! I wondered if she was settling down at school, if she still missed her pony. I hadn't thought about Flora much since I'd got here. There was too much else to think about and too many new people. They were pretty curtains, floral-sprigged in crisp bright colours. Brigid let me take some of the offcuts to sew together, for practice, and I decided to make a quilt for my bed in the Lavender dorm. In Mammy's sewing bag were lots of scraps from things she'd sewed before her death, things I remembered: a blue shirt for Leo, a tartan frock I'd loved, her red apron. I liked the idea of joining them to these new pieces and making something pretty. I liked Brigid better now; she was bossy but patient.

'You can keep it for your bottom drawer,' she said.

'Ugh! I'm never getting married.'

'Och, you say that now.' Brigid touched the ring on her left hand. I supposed she already had a bottom drawer full of household linen and dainty lace, ready for setting up home.

'Are you getting married soon?' I dared to ask.

Brigid sighed. 'I should be married and all by now. Not stuck here. Martin was serving his time at the joinery yard at Harland and Wolff's.' I must have looked blank because she went on, 'The big shipyard. We'd planned to get married when he'd finished his apprenticeship.'

'So why haven't you?'

'He was run out of the yard. Last summer. He hasn't had regular work since. Just casual work at the docks, loading coal, a day here and there. We can't marry on that.'

'What did he do?'

Brigid's voice was low and fierce. 'Nothing,' she said. 'Him and about seven thousand others were run out of the yard because they were Catholics.'

'You might set up home without a man, Polly,' Maggie said, and I guessed she was trying to change the subject out of kindness. 'My auntie lives with her chum. Both their sweethearts died on the first day of the Somme. They were brothers.'

I shuddered. 'Don't talk about the war, Maggie. That's all over now.' *And don't mention brothers.* My cheek was healing now but I could still see Leo's fist coming towards me, the reek of alcohol, the red rage in his face.

I wish you'd died instead of Mammy.

Brigid snorted. 'Not in Belfast. Some of the bastards who marched on the shipyard and put the Catholics out were unemployed ex-servicemen. Full of hate and trained to kill.' She sounded suddenly depressed. 'Right, girls, less talk and more stitching.'

When we went in for lunch, I thought for a moment that Stella had come back, but the girl sitting beside Sandy wasn't her; she was a slim girl with shiny brown hair in a loose bun, and she looked as old as Brigid.

'Edith's here,' Ivy said. 'Sandy'll be pleased.'

'What d'you mean?'

'He's sweet on her.'

'But is he not sweet on Stella?' I asked.

'Stella?' Ivy's voice was full of scorn.

I sat beside Maggie and asked, 'Is Edith a Helen's Hope girl? I haven't seen her before.'

'Sort of. She helps the girls who need a hand reading and writing, and in return Cassie's coaching her for a scholarship to Queen's University. Cassie was a teacher, you see, in a big co-ed school, but at the end of the war she had to give up her job to a returning soldier. She tried to get a job in a girls' school but there were too many women after too few jobs and some of the headmistresses didn't like the fact that she'd taught boys. Thought it wasn't ladylike.' She sniffed in disdain. 'Then she took this house – I think she was left money – and she wanted to do something for girls who hadn't had the chance of an education and then it just grew.'

'And why's it called Helen's Hope? Who's Helen?'

'She was Sandy Reid's cousin. She died on Armistice Day of flu.'

'My mammy died of that flu,' I said. It was the first personal thing I'd told anyone at Helen's Hope.

Maggie nodded. 'It was desperate. My uncle died of it too. Helen was only sixteen,' she went on. 'Cassie'd been her teacher. She says she always remembers Helen talking about a future when people in Ireland could live together without fighting about religion. That's why the hostel is called Helen's Hope. In tribute to her.'

I thought about all the fighting there had been and now Ireland being carved up, and wondered what Helen would think about that.

All through lunch I kept an eye on Sandy and Edith, and when it was time to take my plate to the trolley I lingered over the task, trying to see them up close. They were talking intently and once or twice their laughter rang out. I'd never heard Sandy laugh before. I supposed he was handsome enough if you overlooked the fact that one of his eyes was obviously blind. And of course people would overlook that: it meant he had been a soldier and been wounded. Not like Leo who had come out without a scratch. He was luckier than Maggie's auntie's sweetheart and his brother, killed together at the Somme. Luckier than the men who had marched on the shipyard. Or the men they'd chased from their jobs.

I hadn't known there was so much unemployment. Maybe that was why Sandy was glad of a manual job at Helen's Hope, even though he'd been an officer. He would easily find a sweetheart. Maybe he already had. I narrowed my eyes, watching him with Edith. I didn't think she was as attractive as Stella. Stella was all brightness and movement, her face animated, her bobbed hair golden and swinging. (I tried not to think of her still and white and bleeding.) Edith was pale and slight. Her features were regular and neat, more so than Stella's. But Stella was – well, she was marvellous! She was all fight and passion; she was like the sun and Edith was like the moon.

A singsong voice interrupted my thoughts. 'Polly's got a pa-ash. Polly's got a pa-ash.'

My face flamed and I shoved the dirty plate on to the trolley, plonking the cutlery into the bucket so hard that soapy water splashed out.

'Polly's got a pa-ash.'

'Take that back, Ivy,' I said. 'I have not!' But I knew my cheeks must give me away. Did I have a pash? It was true I'd taken a shine to Stella – just as I'd once lingered in the lanes round Mullankeen hoping to catch a glimpse of Flora on her pony. Just as, before that, I'd idolised Leo. But that was a long time ago.

'Och, never worry yourself,' Ivy said. 'We've all got a wee bit of a pash on Sandy. Nothing to be ashamed of.'

Some of the girls giggled and made swooning gestures, and I giggled too. It was the easiest thing to do.

Chapter 11

I ONLY understood what Helen's Hope was really about at my first weekly meeting. After tea we cleared away as usual and then the dining room was rearranged so that everyone was looking at the front of the room where Cassie, Scottie and Brigid sat looking serious. Edith was beside them, so I guessed she was quite important at Helen's Hope. Expectation fizzed; there had been a great deal of fustling and chatter during tea and several places were empty apart from Stella's – Agnes, Maisie and Tessa, who all worked in a lemonade factory east of here.

'There's trouble,' Maggie said. She always seemed to know what was going on. I'd seen her reading newspapers in the common room when everyone else was happy with the *Girl's Own Paper* or gossip. 'Someone was shot at a march on the way to the Oval football ground and that sparked more shooting and rioting.'

'It's around Short Strand,' Ivy said. 'They probably can't get past.'

I closed my ears. Helen's Hope should be an oasis away from the troubled city and country. I didn't want to remember the sadness on Brigid's face when she told me about her Martin being put out of the shipyard, or the shrieks that had wakened me last night from the room next door and that Tessa said was Agnes having a nightmare about her father being shot dead by the IRA. 'She does it all the time,' she said, and pulled her pillow over her head. 'I wish she'd do it more quietly.' I tried not to look at Catherine, or think about Jamie McMahon and the IRA.

But at the meeting I had to face up to the fact that there was a war on and an election looming and trouble not far away.

At first it was dull. Scottie said there was an outbreak of measles in the local elementary school and we were to avoid cutting through it as a shortcut to the tram stop.

Brigid was asked to give a report on the factory. She stood up, blushing slightly, and said it had been a mixed week.

'We did the order for the orphanage, and we're working on the curtains for Ellis House,' she said, 'but then the order book's empty. Unless something's come in that I don't know about, with Stella out of action?' Her voice rose uncertainly and Cassie shook her head. Ivy looked from one to the other with an expression I couldn't read – puzzled or disappointed?

'No orders,' Cassie said. 'At least – none we can accept. But we've advertised in the papers this week, so hopefully ...'

Ivy put her hand up and without being invited asked, 'What do you mean none we can accept?' Some of the girls around her murmured their support and I could feel Maggie and Catherine tense on either side of me.

69

Cassie sighed. 'Nothing you need bother about, Ivy.'

'No, she has a point,' Scottie said. 'Ivy, you know the ethos of Helen's Hope.' She went on, as if quoting, 'Helen's Hope is a community founded on the principles of non-sectarianism and co-operation. We seek to work for peace and harmony. That being so, it's against our philosophy to promote anything which might incite bigotry or division.' Some of the girls, me included, were looking at her dully. She went on, 'There was an order placed this week' – Ivy looked triumphant – 'from a local – well, organisation. Asking for some union flags. Naturally we were unable to accept it.'

'Why not?' Ivy demanded.

'No flags or emblems,' said a new voice from the back of the room. Everyone turned round and there was Stella. She still looked very pale, but she was dressed and looked as determined as ever. My heart gave the same little skip it used to do when I saw Flora.

'Stella! You shouldn't be out of bed!' Scottie said.

'I'm fine,' Stella said. 'I guessed this would come up. I couldn't let you discuss it without me.'

'We're quite capable,' Cassie said, at the same time as Scottie said, 'Well, for goodness sake come and sit down,' and Ivy said, 'You're not the boss of us.'

'Shut up, Ivy,' I said. A few people looked shocked and I heard someone say, 'Oooh! Listen to the new girl!' Ivy narrowed her eyes at me.

Stella made her way to the front of the room. She took the chair Edith offered and carried on speaking as if there had been no interruption. 'We're certainly not dealing with the kind of organisation who placed that order. Or tried to.'

'What about the banners we made for the Women's International League of Peace and Freedom?' Ivy demanded. 'That's one of the biggest orders we've had.'

'And those flags for the Trade Union gala,' someone cut in.

'You didn't ask any of us if we agreed with the organisations,' Ivy said.

'It's completely different,' Stella snapped.

'No, it's not,' said more than one girl.

I wished I could join in, on Stella's side of course, but I was far too ignorant.

'The union flag is the flag of this country,' Ivy said, her voice wavering but growing stronger as some of the girls started to protest. 'Yes, it is! Ulster is British and thank God it's staying that way whatever those eejits and gunmen think.'

There was uproar at this. Catherine wriggled in her seat, and I thought about Agnes's father being shot by the IRA, remembered the graffiti on our shop in Mullankeen and Stella being hurt because of a flag being raised somewhere it wasn't welcome.

Ivy raised her voice above the tumult. 'If we're being offered good money to make banners and flags we should take it. Or' – with a sly glance at Stella who everyone knew was a passionate suffragist – 'at least vote on it.' She flashed a look round us all. I could sense the room breaking into factions, and it was not as simple as Catholic and Protestant. I didn't think all the Protestant girls would agree with Ivy. She wasn't exactly popular: people were wary of her, rather than liking her. Some might disagree out of principle, because the ethos – what was that word Cassie had used? – the *philosophy* of Helen's Hope mattered to them. Girls like Maggie. And maybe some of the Catholic girls wouldn't mind what they made, if it brought more money in to Helen's Hope?

'Personally I'd rather chop my fingers off than use them to sew British flags,' a girl called Winifred said, and there was a cheer from one or two of the mill girls. Ivy flushed and I remembered her own mutilated finger.

'And, Ivy, you wouldn't like it if you were asked to make Irish tricolours or banners for Sinn Féin, would you?' Edith spoke for the first time.

Ivy snorted. 'That's not going to happen!'

'Why not?'

'Because this is a Protestant area. The people who asked us wanted to keep it local. They were doing us a favour.'

'How do you know who asked us?' Stella said, her face severe. She looked at Cassie, who frowned.

Ivy tossed her plait. 'I'm from these streets. I talk to people. I'm not a do-gooder blow-in thinking I know better than people who've been born and reared here for generations.'

Why did Ivy live in Helen's Hope, I wondered, if she came from round here?

Stella half stood up and then swayed and sank back down, closing her eyes briefly. Edith, beside her, gave her shoulder a brief comforting rub.

Cassie raised a warning hand. 'Ivy, you forget yourself,' she said quietly. 'This is not exclusively a Protestant area. It is still mixed. And in the past this area had good community relations. We must do what we can to promote what's left of that. And making partisan, inflammatory emblems – of whatever hue – is not the way to do so.'

'But it's the flag of this country,' Ivy said.

'A flag which is being used to taunt our Catholic neighbours,' Cassie said. 'It was flown from the Catholic church last summer – a despicable act of provocation.' Then she became less patient. 'For goodness' sake, Ivy, this city is erupting in violence nearly every night of the week. Flags are being waved and burned all over the place. We at Helen's Hope will never add to that. Now, everyone, listen to me. There will be no vote. This is not up for further discussion. Stella will write and say that we cannot accept their order and that will be an end to the matter.'

The words were confident, and so was her voice, but I think we all knew that it wasn't an end to the matter at all.

Chapter 12

'COME out to the garden,' Catherine said. 'It might calm us down.'

I followed her outside. The soft evening sun was warming the old red brick of the garden wall. Some early roses were blooming, pale pink. I caught wafts of their scent. It seemed a world away from the disquiet of the meeting, yet I could hear some girls still arguing through an open window, and in the distance the roar of a riot on an unknown street.

'Are meetings always like that?'

Catherine shook her head. 'Normally we just vote on things like should we take the *Girl's Own Paper* or if the girls who work long hours in the mill should do less housework.' Her voice changed. 'Oooh,' she said, 'Sandy's here. He must have stayed to walk Edith home after the meeting.'

He was on his knees, raking a bare bed of earth. A box of small plants stood beside him, their roots bare and fragile, like tiny bones.

'Hello, Sandy,' Catherine said and gave him a shy grin. Her eyes looked very blue and bright. I sighed. It was just the way she used to look at Jamie McMahon. She didn't seem able to help herself. But I thought of how my heart skipped when I saw Stella, exactly like it used to with Flora. Maybe I was just as bad. Having pashes on girls was all right in school stories; I wasn't sure if you were allowed them in real life.

'Well, Catherine. Meeting over already?' Sandy looked at his watch.

'Yes. We can help if you like.'

'Can I trust you not to plant these upside down?' He looked at me with a flicker of recognition. 'How are you settling in?' he asked.

'All right. How's your arm?' I asked.

'Fine. D'you know much about gardening?'

I shook my head.

'Make sure they aren't too close together. They need room to grow. I want to get Edith home as soon as I can. By all accounts there's trouble all over the east of the city.' He sounded worried.

'She's on the summer seat with Stella,' Tessa said.

'Is Stella up?'

'Scottie tried to make her go back to bed,' I said, 'but she wanted fresh air.'

Sandy set off. The summer seat was just behind the greenhouse at the bottom of the garden. You could see it through the glass but sort of distorted, like book illustrations under tissue paper. I could just make out Edith and Stella sitting together. We watched him go towards the greenhouse in the far corner. A few other girls came out and sat around in groups chatting, including Tessa, Agnes and Maisie, shrill and rumpled. I guessed they would have lurid tales of the trouble they'd battled through to get home from the factory. I didn't want to hear, and I didn't want Catherine to go running after Tessa. It felt nice to be doing something with Catherine. I didn't see her at all during the day and in the evenings she had work to prepare for college, which involved a lot of sighing and chewing of her fingernails in the common room. She was much happier in the garden doing something practical. She kept looking up towards the summer seat.

'Sandy's awful handsome, isn't he?' she said.

I shrugged.

'He reminds me of Leo, before –'

'Ugh. Don't.' I changed the subject. 'Is he sweet on Stella? Or Edith? Or both?'

Catherine paused in her digging and pondered. 'I think Edith,' she said. 'Stella's too …' She wrinkled her nose.

'D'you not like her?' I felt stung.

Catherine gouged another hole into the soil and eyed it narrowly to check it was the right distance from its neighbour.

'Course I like her,' she said. 'She's the heart of this place. She works harder than anyone I've ever met. But she's so energetic sometimes she makes me exhausted. Like, I'll be wanting to lie on my bed and just relax or do my hair or something and she'll want to talk about women's rights or hand out leaflets or …' She ground to a halt and then said, 'I don't want to improve my mind. I just want a quiet life.'

'You wouldn't have had a quiet life with Jamie McMahon.'

Catherine fluttered a hand in front of her eyes. 'Oh, Poll, don't! Can we not just, you know, draw a line under all that?'

I shrugged. 'If you want.'

For a while we didn't speak much. Catherine made the holes and I plopped the plants in and we both patted the earth round them to make them secure. It was nice being with Catherine. My hands busied themselves in the cool earth but my mind was drifting nowhere in particular. The last of the evening sun moved round to find us, in our little spot in front of the potting shed; I enjoyed the glow of it on my neck and every so often I'd look up and see it glinting on Stella's fair hair.

A crash burst through the air. Catherine and I jumped.

'What the –!'

Someone started to scream, on and on. Someone else shouted, 'Shut up!'

Catherine said, 'It's the greenhouse! It's been hit – look!'

'Stella's there!'

We started to run. A few other girls were running too but we got there first. The greenhouse had a jagged hole in its side. Glass lay in shards around it. Sandy, Edith and Stella didn't seem hurt, though Stella had some splinters of glass stuck to her skirt. I was so relieved Stella was all right, though what a waste that I hadn't been the one to rescue her.

Catherine bent down and lifted half a brick from the path. 'This must be what did it.'

Stella shuddered. 'Looks like the other half of the one that got me the other day,' she said.

'Really?' I asked. 'How can you –?'

She sighed. 'Not really. One brick looks much like another.'

'You could all have been killed,' Catherine said.

'We're fine,' Edith said.

'Stella, stay still.' Sandy bent and carefully pulled the splinters off her skirt. His fingers left traces of soil behind on the pale blue fabric and one of the shards grazed his fingertip but he just rubbed it on his trousers. We all looked at the jagged, heavy brick and I thought of Stella a few days ago, the blood tangling her hair and staining Sandy's sleeve.

The other girls were hovering.

'Get rid of them, will you?' Edith said. 'We don't need people fussing.'

I turned to the others. 'It's nothing.' I held up the brick. 'I dislodged this old brick with my spade and it flew across the path and broke a pane in the greenhouse.'

'Polly doesn't know her own strength,' Edith said lightly.

The girls muttered and exclaimed and some of them ragged me about being clumsy, but gradually they drifted back to work in their own parts of the garden. But Catherine and I stayed.

'Why did you lie?' Catherine asked me. 'You know someone threw that brick over the wall.'

'Youngsters,' Stella said. 'Eejits. We don't need to scare the girls.' She looked at me approvingly and I glowed.

'Youngsters and eejits can hurt people,' Edith said. 'As you know better than anyone.'

'Why would someone attack Helen's Hope?' Catherine asked. She sounded as scared as I felt, but I hoped I was better at hiding it.

Stella sighed. 'Some people can't stand the idea of people of different faiths living together. They think we'll – I don't know – contaminate each other. And then – well! We're all women. Daring to live without men, so stands to reason we must all be witches and Jezebels.'

'Ridiculous when Cassie has us living like nuns, practically,' Catherine said.

'There's plenty round here would throw bricks at us if we were nuns,' Stella said.

'So we can't win?' I asked.

Stella nodded. 'It'd never have been easy, setting up a community like this. Even somewhere like Manchester, where I grew up. Somewhere normal. But in Belfast right now, with the whole place like a bag of weasels, we must be crazy.' She gave a sudden grin. 'Lucky we're not scared of a challenge.' She reached out and ruffled my hair and because it was Stella I didn't mind. 'Don't look so worried, Polly. It'll be all right. There's been trouble since that march to the Oval. It'll just be the aftermath of that. Sandy's right – it's only youngsters.'

'This time,' Edith said.

'There won't be a next time,' Stella said.

I wished I believed her.

Chapter 13

'PROMISE you'll be careful,' Cassie said as Brigid, Catherine and I and a handful of others gathered in the hall on Sunday morning.

'You didn't say that to the Protestants,' I said. We had watched girls leave to go to the Church of Ireland church, to the Methodists, the Presbyterians, and to the tin-roofed gospel hall. And some girls went nowhere: everyone was free to worship where – and if – they wanted.

Cassie looked worried. 'You know how things are. Don't draw attention to yourselves.'

Catherine couldn't help drawing attention to herself. She didn't mean to, she crept around quietly, but she was so pretty, especially in her good Sunday frock, her curls fizzing from under her soft felt hat, that people would always look at her. The other girls, Winifred and Mary, walked in front, chatting.

When I'd realised that I didn't have to go to Mass, I was tempted not to. At home you weren't let off unless you were half-dying. Or unless you were Leo, of course. But the habit was so ingrained, the duty to hear Mass every

Sunday drummed into me by Mammy and Daddy and the nuns. Catherine would have had kittens if I'd suggested not going. And Mammy – she'd be turning in her grave. I'd always liked the music. The convent had a choir which sang the responses and anthems and you could lose yourself in that and forget any connection between the high, disembodied, sweet voices from the gallery and the harsh bark of Sister Mary Aloysius saying Polly McCabe was an affront to Catholic girlhood and was going to the bad quicker than our poor Blessed Lady could intercede for her. I looked forward to the music in Belfast, to burying my head in my hands and giving thanks for this chance, and for Stella being all right and not mentioning what I'd done to attract that brick to her head. I could pray for Daddy not to be too lonely without me.

I didn't plan to pray for Leo.

The clock above Kennedy's shop showed five to eleven.

'Hurry up,' I said. 'I don't want to have to stand for the whole Mass.'

Catherine laughed. 'Don't worry. You'll have no problem getting a seat.'

I assumed she meant because the church was so big. In Mullankeen the chapel was small and always packed. The Catholic church on the main road not far from Helen's Hope was a large grey stone building, with a tall tower and a big Celtic cross in front of it. That cross made me feel at home, as did the smell of incense when Brigid pushed open the front door and led us into the porch. As I blessed myself with holy water I was surprised at how comforted

81

I was by the familiar ritual. But in the dim church I knew what Catherine had meant. There was room for several hundred people but most of the pews were half-empty, people spread out like currants in a fruit scone. At first I thought we had mistaken the time, but no, the bell was tolling. If the congregation had all gone together to the front they would have taken up only four or five rows; I wasn't sure if that would have looked better or worse. I supposed people sat where they'd always sat. I wondered where all the other people had gone to, and why.

There was no choir, and the young priest sounded very different from Father O'Kane at home, sort of impatient; maybe it was his Belfast accent. Only the Mass itself was the same. It should have been comforting, but as I looked round the half-empty church through my fingers when I was meant to be praying after communion, I couldn't help shivering. The noon sun was shining through the stained-glass windows behind the altar but the space was too big and dark for it to make much light.

When we came out of the chapel a group of boys was hanging round the gate. One of them gobbed out a big spit that landed on Catherine's coat. I went to run at him but Brigid grabbed my arm. 'Don't,' she said. 'Just ignore it. They're only youngsters.'

The spit soaked into Catherine's coat. I thought about Stella's blood soaking into Sandy's sleeve, and the brick that had shattered the greenhouse. *They're only youngsters.*

I couldn't help looking back. They were walking behind us, and the one who had spat started to work his lips like he was about to do it again. He was about seventeen, with a duncher cap on his head. Old enough to know better. I rushed on, the same anger swelling in me that I'd felt the day I'd arrived. I knew if his spit landed on me I'd fly back and thump him. I'd pull the stupid cap off his head and dash it to the gutter. And then there'd really be trouble. Brawling in the street! I imagined Stella saying, 'That is against the spirit of Helen's Hope!' But surely it wasn't in the spirit of Helen's Hope to let people jeer at you?

'Fenian hoors. Taigs.'

I spun round, but Brigid dug her fingers into my arm and dragged me along with her. 'Don't make it worse,' she said quietly. 'Never let on you hear them. They're just stupid wee bigots. Looking for a row.'

'It's awful low,' Winifred said. 'And us with the blessed sacrament hardly down our throats.'

Unease prickled me. There hadn't been a crowd at Mass, but even so, dozens of people had left the church. Why pick on us? Because we were girls? Or because we were part of Helen's Hope?

We were all arm-in-arm now, bustling along, trying not to run, trying not to act nervous. The boys kept behind us, and the taunts kept coming.

'Brigid,' I said. 'If we go straight back they'll know where we come from. They might ...' I remembered the brick smashing through the greenhouse.

Brigid sounded weary. 'I'm sure they know fine rightly where we're from. But let's juke in here for a bit. She always opens for a couple of hours on a Sunday morning.' She nodded at Kennedy's shop.

The shop bell jangled loudly when we opened the door, and the woman behind the counter thrust her arms over the till. 'Oh,' she said, looking relieved. 'When I saw such a crowd I thought ... These days you can't be too careful.'

'Miss Kennedy, we haven't come in to buy,' Brigid said.

Miss Kennedy looked alarmed.

'I mean,' Brigid explained, 'some hallions were following us from Mass, saying ... och, you know, teasing us, and some of the girls were upset' – Catherine duly went big eyed and pathetic looking – 'so I thought we should come in here and let them get past.'

It was dim inside the shop, partly because the window was crowded with tin adverts for Fry's chocolate and Gallaher's cigarettes and Lyons tea, and partly because it was criss-crossed with strips of brown paper. I guessed this was to protect it from bricks and stones. I thought of our own shop at home, and Daddy scrubbing off the graffiti.

'Yous did right.' Miss Kennedy leaned over the counter. Her bosom rested on her folded arms. 'For dear sake, it's come to something when wee bits of girls can't get home from Mass in peace. I don't know how much longer I can keep going here myself. Between the threats and ... och, sure, never mind that.' She reached to the shelves behind her and took down a jar of chocolate toffee rolls. She unscrewed it, unleashing a gorgeous smell of toffee, and offered it round. 'A wee sweet won't put yous off your lunch, will it? Were there many out? There was hardly a sinner at eight o'clock.' She tutted. 'Poor Father Byrne's heart-scared he'll be sent where there's more need for him. Sure there's hardly a Catholic left in these streets.'

'There's more need for dear Father Byrne here than ever,' Winifred said piously and pinkly. I'd noticed her rapt face at Communion and couldn't help wondering if her bliss was all about the blessed sacrament. Father Byrne was young and Catherine said he looked like Buster Keaton. I bit down on my toffee and the chocolate exploded into my mouth. I tried to chew it slowly to make it last. I'd been given five shillings for my week's work. It was token pocket money – I was getting my board and my training – but it was my first proper wages. All the skivvying I'd done at home had been for nothing; it was just expected of me because I was a girl. Sometimes Daddy gave me sixpence for myself but this money felt more mine. I could spend it all on chocolate toffee rolls if I wanted.

The shop bell jangled again and Miss Kennedy looked tense and then relaxed. 'Och, Mrs McKee,' she said. 'Your usual?'

We took that as our cue to leave. The street outside was Sunday-still, a warm breeze scuttling a Bourneville chocolate-bar wrapper down the gutter and the noon sun hot in the hair at my neck. I didn't have it as tightly bound as I did for the factory but it felt damp and itchy. I thought of Stella's swinging bob and Maggie's neat shingle.

'Catherine,' I said, 'would you help me with something after lunch?'

She raised her eyebrows. 'Give me a clue?'

Brigid was in front and for all I knew what I planned was against the rules. I made my fingers into a scissor shape and mimed cutting my hair.

Catherine's eyes widened. 'Miss Catherine Daly, coiffeuse to the stars,' she said, just as we turned the corner and followed Brigid down the alley we always used as a shortcut.

I was about to tell her to shush when a shadow fell across the path.

'Trying to avoid us?' It was the boy in the duncher cap and his henchmen. They spread themselves across the narrow alley so we couldn't pass. On either side loomed the high brick walls of back yards. My heart bashed at my chest wall and I seemed to feel my toffee lodged in my gullet. Brigid stepped in front to take charge. She was older and taller than him – she was about twenty, for goodness' sake – but even though he had to look up at her there was contempt in his face and confidence in his shoulders. He folded his arms across his chest and that's when I recognised him as the boy with the flag from the other night. Maybe the boy who'd hurt Stella. Certainly the boy who'd started it all.

'Let us past,' Brigid said, her voice calm but a dark mottled red creeping up the back of her neck under her neat hair. The boys laughed and swaggered their shoulders so that they were taking up even more space. The sun glinted on some glass splinters on the ground.

Catherine tried to make a dash for it, but one of them grabbed her arm and shook her. The bud of anger in me, dormant for days, burst into bloom. How dare this spotty youth treat Catherine like this! How dare the whole stupid lot of them try and stop us getting home! I realised that for the first time I was thinking of Helen's Hope as home. I dug my elbow hard into his armpit. He gave a yip of pain and Catherine wrestled free.

'Don't you dare touch my cousin,' I said. 'This is a free country. We'll walk down this alley if we want.'

'I don't think yous will. Fraser' – he appealed to the leader – 'you see what she done on me?'

'Fenian witch,' Fraser said. 'Ugly too. Is that a scouring pad on your head?' To my shame I felt my eyes burn with tears. 'Free country, is it? Not for the likes of yous. Yous wait till the election on Tuesday. We'll get rid of fenian scum. This is a Protestant state for Protestant people.'

'Aye, in your dreams.' Catherine sounded so fierce that I was shocked. 'There's bigger men than you prepared to fight for Ireland. We'll see whose country it is then.' I wondered if she was thinking about Jamie. I wondered if these were Jamie's words.

He spat at the word 'Ireland'. 'Away yous go over the border to your own sort.'

'Sort?' I asked. 'What sort would that be? *People?*' I remembered what Stella had said the other night.

'Fenians. Taigs. Catholics.' And then he said something strange. 'Too good to make our flags?' His eyes narrowed. 'We'll see about that.'

We looked at each other in confusion. What did he know about that?

'You Prods are all the same,' I yelled back. 'Bigoted bastards. Thinking you own the place. It's our country too.'

87

I hadn't known those words were in me. I hadn't realised I could sound so bitter. All the anger I'd had curled up in me since Leo came home and Mammy died centred on these jeering boys in a Belfast back street.

The words came easily but even as they spewed from my mouth I knew they weren't the right words. I didn't hate them because they were Protestants. I hated them because they hated us. And I hated Fraser especially for his insults. *Ugly. Scouring pad.*

Pounding footsteps behind the boys. Stella, with no hat on, her face outraged.

'What the hell are you doing?' she demanded. 'Isn't there enough trouble in this city without neighbours shouting at neighbours?' I didn't know if she was angry at Fraser's gang or at us. At me: I was the one yelling insults.

Fraser swung round. He looked up and down Stella's tall figure and jeered. 'What would you know?' Did he know her? Did he know she was the same girl he'd left lying in a pool of blood the other night? Did he care? There was something about the way they all looked at us that was disturbing – they hated us for being Catholics, certainly, but they hated us more for being girls. Girls who were standing up for themselves.

When Sandy came round the corner, tall, broad, every inch the army officer, Fraser gulped and looked less brave, and his henchmen shuffled.

'Picking on a crowd of girls?' Sandy asked, his voice pleasant and steady but a little tremor in his jaw showing his anger. He looked them up and down and under his critical gaze they became a pathetic ragbag. 'Away home to your mammies.'

Muttering, they drifted apart, let us past, though Fraser gave me a dig in the ribs as I pushed by him. 'Yous'll be hearing from my Uncle Alec,' he said, his voice wet in my ear, his breath smoky.

'Your Uncle Alec can go to hell,' I said, and dug him back.

'Polly!' Stella said, catching up with me as I stalked down the street. 'You can't behave like that!'

'They started it!'

'You shouldn't have insulted them. You shouldn't have used that kind of language. Bigoted –'

'They called us –'

'We're meant to be better than that.'

Catherine opened her mouth – to stand up for me, I assumed – but Stella held up her hand.

'No,' she said. 'I don't want to hear it. I'll have to talk to Cassie. She sent me out to find you, you were so late home from Mass. We thought there must be trouble but we didn't expect this.'

Winifred began to cry. 'Shut up,' Brigid said. She seemed flustered since Stella turned up; maybe she was embarrassed at not keeping us under better control.

'You can't blame us, Stella,' I said. 'We were minding our own business. They started on us. What were we meant to do – just take it?'

'No. I don't know.' It wasn't like Stella to sound so unsure.

Sandy took her arm. 'You're still not yourself,' he began but she shook his arm off.

She sounded – but it was impossible, not Stella! – almost in tears. 'Don't patronise me!' She stalked off on her own.

Sandy looked at us and gave an embarrassed sort of shrug. 'I'll just see you all safely home,' he said.

Catherine beamed. 'Our hero.'

'You got rid of them,' Brigid said. Which was the truth, but I wondered if it was one of the reasons Stella seemed so annoyed. And what about the flags? There was more going on than I understood.

Chapter 14

I COULD hardly eat my lunch and as I was clearing my plate I saw Stella and Cassie deep in conversation.

'What'll they do to us?' Catherine asked fearfully.

I shrugged. 'Rap our knuckles? Throw us out? Feed us to next door's pig?' I didn't feel as bold as I sounded. I wished Maggie was here with her solid good sense and calm way of looking at things, but she'd gone home for the day. 'We only stood up for ourselves. There's no point in looking like that, Catherine. Cassie'll send for us when she sends for us. We might as well enjoy ourselves first. It's a lovely day. Maybe we could go to the park?' I remembered hearing that Ellis House, where Flora was at school, was near the park, and I thought we could go and have a nosy.

But before we were out of the room an order went up from Cassie: everyone was to stay within bounds. 'There's a big nationalist rally on today and we all know how tensions can spread.' Ivy snorted in disgust. I heard one or two girls mutter, 'Those Catholics! Why should we suffer?'

Catherine grabbed my arm. 'Let's go into the garden,' she said. 'And what did you say about cutting your hair?'

'What about your hair?' Ivy demanded.

'It gets in the way when I'm sewing. Catherine's going to help me cut it.'

Ivy's eyes widened. 'Are you mad? She's so clumsy. She'll probably cut your ears off.'

'Well, that'd be a blessing if I didn't have to listen to you.' Until then I'd been dubious about letting Catherine loose with the scissors, but there was no way I was going to let Ivy get away with that.

Ivy tossed her own hair, which she wore loose today, the front tied back with a frayed blue ribbon. 'She can hardly make it any worse,' she said and walked off.

Catherine looked uncertain. 'Maybe Tessa would be better doing it,' she said. 'She's good at that kind of thing.'

'No. It has to be you.' I didn't like to admit that I was jealous of Catherine being so friendly with Tessa.

Catherine, hairbrush and comb in her frock pocket, took me to the far end of the garden, behind the greenhouse. I was carrying my good dressmaking scissors and my quilt. I didn't know if cutting hair was against the rules, but if anyone challenged us I would say I was going to sew.

'Not here,' I said. 'People can see.'

But Catherine knew the garden better than I did. She led me behind a big escallonia bush, and it felt like we were in our own green world. She dragged an old chair with her, and I sat down. She stood behind me and started to unpin my hair and brush it. Nobody had brushed my hair since Mammy died. I closed my eyes, enjoying it in a slightly wistful way.

'And what would Madam like today?' Catherine asked.

'Oh, help! Do I really want to do this?' I asked. 'Maybe just tidy it up a bit?'

'I thought Madam wanted a fashionable short style?'

I giggled – she sounded so like a real hairdresser, not that I'd ever been to one. Mammy used to cut my hair but it hadn't been cut for two years. Auntie May had offered more than once, saying I looked like a Highland cow, but stubbornness had always made me refuse.

'I don't know!'

'Well, Madam might like the fashionable bob, but the shingle is becoming very popular with the really modern miss.' She ran her hands through my dry, frizzy hair. It crackled with electricity. 'Ow! Your hair stung me!'

I squeezed my eyes shut and handed her the scissors. 'Just cut,' I said.

At first the scissors pecked at me nervously and only tiny wisps of gingery hair floated to the ground.

'For goodness' sake, Catherine, we'll be here all day.'

'I'm scared of making a mess. I'm not really sure ...'

'Oh, just do it! You'll be grand.' I sounded more confident than I felt, but before I knew what was happening she had grabbed my hair into one long straggle, placed the scissors at the nape of my neck – I shivered at the cold steel – and chopped. A rush of air at my neck and ...

'There you go.' She sounded slightly scared.

I ran my hands through what was left of my hair. It felt soft and light and strange. No longer a scouring pad. But short. Very, very short. The cut-off tail coiled on the grass like a hairy ginger snake.

'Can you tidy it up?' I suggested. 'I don't suppose it's a real shingle just like that?'

'N-no. But shorter than a bob. More of a bingle.'

'Well, make it look proper,' I said. 'Like Maggie's.'

'Um.' Catherine sounded more uncertain than ever. 'I'll try.' The scissors stabbed my neck. Little huffs of hair floated down round me onto the grass. It seemed to take a long time.

'Catherine – stop.' I ran my hand up the back of my head. It felt rough and prickly. I wriggled away and spun round to face her. She looked more scared than when the boy had grabbed her. What on earth had she done to me? I heard Fraser's voice again: *Ugly*. And Ivy: *She can't make it any worse*.

'It's not quite even,' Catherine admitted. She brandished the scissors. 'I need to –'

'You need to get me your hand-mirror,' I said. I put my hands protectively over my head.

'Oh. I forgot it. But you'll need two to see the back of your head. You'd better go up and look in the glass in our room.'

'I'm going nowhere until I see what I look like.' I could imagine running into Cassie. Or Stella. I'd hate Stella to see me looking a fright.

'But one mirror's no good.'

'Well, run up and get mine too!'

'Aye aye, captain.' She saluted and turned to go.

'Leave the scissors,' I said.

She handed them to me, and while she was gone I picked up the quilt to distract myself from worrying about my hair. It was starting to look pretty; the fabric from the girls' school curtains was much nicer than anything I'd ever worked with before. Lucky girls, lucky Flora, waking up to blue-sprigged cotton, or those tiny pink roses, and the yellow one was nice too – were they tulips or fat daffodils? And mixed up with the new floral fabric were patches of the old things I had found in the sewing bag. My quilt would be a mix of old and new, and it would be the prettiest thing I'd ever owned. Then only Ivy would be the odd one out, with her plain grey blanket. And serve her right.

I spread out what I'd done, threaded my needle and started to sew. It felt lovely to be hand sewing again after the stressful hours on the machine. It reminded me of being with Mammy, and for once I let myself remember that. It took my mind off my nerves about my hair and what Cassie would say about the encounter in the street. It almost helped me not to think about that interview with her on the first morning. *You're very much on trial, Polly. If we have any doubts about your influence...* She hadn't finished the sentence; she hadn't needed to.

Catherine was taking for ever! It wasn't against the rules to go up to the dorms during the day, but maybe she'd been stopped by Cassie for her interview; maybe she was even now in Cassie's study, getting a wigging. *Wigging.* How appropriate! I'd thought she'd interview us together but maybe she was taking us one by one. I imagined Catherine's bright nervous eyes and fiery hair subdued by Cassie's disgust. And Catherine hadn't been anything like as bad as me. Catherine wasn't on trial.

Chapter 15

IT was quiet in the garden, a lazy May afternoon with bees humming and just the occasional calls and giggles. Beyond the wall, in the street, the rhythmic thump of ball against kerb and the shrill voices of children. Nothing, for now, more sinister. Then I became aware of deeper voices, much closer to me, on the other side of the escallonia bush. Stella and Sandy. I froze. I didn't want to eavesdrop but I couldn't creep out looking like this. Then I heard my name and I couldn't stop myself listening.

'Polly was the worst,' Stella said. 'I could have swung for her. Honestly, Sandy, if I'd known what a firebrand she was I wouldn't have persuaded Cassie to give her a chance. She was dubious from the start. She's so unlike Catherine; Catherine's a mouse.'

My cheeks burned with indignation. I'd rather be a firebrand than a mouse!

'She opens her mouth without thinking,' Stella went on.

A gulp caught in my throat; I couldn't believe they wouldn't hear it. But Sandy's next words, obviously meant to calm Stella, settled me a bit.

'You're over-reacting. Come on, Stella, you'd be the first to shout back at someone! When have you ever kept quiet when you had something to say? She must have felt scared of those boys, and when people are scared they lash out.'

Like Leo. His fist looming. Lashing out. But he wasn't scared; he was just horrible.

She opens her mouth without thinking.

But when I said – what I said – to Leo, I hadn't said it without thinking. I'd said it deliberately. To hurt him.

I wish you'd never come home. I wish you'd died instead of Mammy. You killed her anyway.

Stella gave a long sigh. 'Why are you so reasonable?' she said. 'It's really annoying.'

A quick sharp laugh. 'Reasonable? Would you tell my mother that, please?'

'More trouble?' Her voice was sympathetic.

'The usual. She hates me working here. When are you going to get a real job? What am I supposed to tell my friends? Doing manual labour for those –'

Stella joined in. 'Those terrible modern women! It's not –'

'Natural!' they finished at the same time and laughed. But when Sandy spoke again he sounded serious. 'But it's *not* a real job, is it? Cassie can't pay me much.'

'I thought you didn't mind? You said as long as you were out of doors, doing something practical, and not stuck in an office –'

'Yes, but it's not a living wage.'

'But you love it here? You believe in Helen's Hope?' I wasn't sure if Stella was asking him or telling him.

'You've always said you wanted to be involved because of Helen – to honour her memory.'

'I did. I do.' His voice softened. 'Helen would have loved how passionate you all are about trying to make a place – a sort of oasis really – where it doesn't matter what religion you are or if you see yourself as Irish or British.'

'Oasis.' Stella sounded thoughtful. 'That's in the desert, isn't it?'

'Yes. A watering hole.'

'Only sometimes people *think* they see an oasis but they don't. It's only wishful thinking. A mirage.'

'What are you on about?'

'Maybe that's all Helen's Hope is – a mirage. An impossible dream.' Stella's voice was more hopeless than I'd ever heard it. 'Maybe different people can't live together and I'm as naïve as everyone says. Those boys –'

'Youngsters.'

'You keep saying that, but you've seen how close the violence is getting, how these streets are changing. Nobody really wants us here. The Catholics see us as Protestant do-gooders; the Protestants think we're fenian hoors; everybody's suspicious of us. Nobody seems to understand why women would want to live without men. They call us the coven. Maybe we are stupid. The city's seething, the country's at war – and we just sit here making curtains and having meetings about tolerance.'

'Stella.'

She ignored him, and her voice rose. 'And now our own girls brawl in the street like guttersnipes. Honestly, what's the point of it all!'

When Sandy spoke again his voice came from a different place; I imagined that he'd moved closer to Stella and was giving her a hug. 'Don't, Stella. You're always so positive. If *you* give in –'

A long trembling sigh and then a groan. 'I won't give in.'

'Good.'

'But I need to find a way to make Helen's Hope more – I don't know – accepted.'

'If anyone can, you can.'

Stella's voice grew brisk and more like itself. 'So what's this about your mother?'

His turn to sigh. 'She has a point.' He sounded embarrassed. 'Working here was all very well when I first came home. Earn some pocket money, throw Mother a few shillings for my keep.'

'And you do a great job.'

'But it's not enough. No career, no real prospects. But what else can I do? The only thing I've been trained for is to kill people.'

'You're no different from thousands of men your age.' I'd never heard Stella sound so gentle. 'You all came of age in the army. You're better off –'

'You don't have to tell me. Half the boys in my class –'

'I know.'

'You know that fellow who sells matches sometimes on the corner of Castlereagh Street?' Sandy's voice was very serious. 'I talk to him. He's called Patrick Neill. He was a corporal in the Tenth Irish. He's from the Falls Road, but

99

his community's shunned him because he fought in the King's uniform. Called him a traitor to Ireland.'

My heart caught at this. Just like Leo! I didn't want to think about Leo. I didn't want to hear about this soldier. But when you're hiding behind a bush and eavesdropping you don't get to choose what you hear.

'He lives in a hostel in the city,' Sandy went on, 'and he walks out to different areas to sell his matches because he's scared to show his face in his own streets. But round here he's scared people will find out he's a Catholic. He can't bloody win. He gave his youth, his right arm, his *sanity* for their bloody war and now he's not safe in his own city.'

'Sandy,' Stella said. 'I know. I agree. That's why I'm working in Helen's Hope instead of changing the world in London or enjoying myself at home. But why are you so frustrated about it now?'

'Because I want to get married. And I can't keep a wife on what I earn here.'

My breath caught again. This was much too private for me to be listening to, but I couldn't blunder out and show myself now. And where on earth was Catherine?

'Married?' Stella's voice was uncertain. 'You mean Edith?'

'Of course Edith. Who else would I want to marry?'

Until now I had had no idea how Stella felt about Sandy. How could I? For all I had a sort of pash on Stella, I barely knew her. But I could hear the hurt in her voice. There was no mistaking it. I could almost feel the arrows pierce her heart. How could Sandy not notice? I hardly dared breathe. Would she pretend she didn't mind? Would she be able to sound pleased for them and hide the fact that she was in love with Sandy herself? I was so tense waiting for her next words. And when they came I had no doubts – she was heartbroken! But being Stella she wasn't going to show it. At least, she wasn't going to cry and plead. Her voice was tight and proud and I didn't think Sandy would guess that it was on the edge of tears. But *I* knew.

'Does Edith know about this – this plan?' she asked. 'I mean' – a tiny bit of hope crept into her voice – 'have you asked her? Has she said yes?'

Silence. I supposed he was nodding. Or, no, shaking his head, because her next words were, 'Well, don't you think you should?'

'We don't get much chance to be alone.'

'There's no point worrying how to support a wife if you haven't even asked her. She might say no.' Did she sound hopeful?

I didn't find out Sandy's reaction to that, because next minute I heard Stella say, loud and surprised, 'Catherine? Where are you going?'

I might be a firebrand but I wasn't a beast and I couldn't leave poor Catherine to dither and panic without me, so I stepped out of my hiding place to face the row.

Chapter 16

STELLA and Sandy looked at me in shock, Catherine in obvious relief.

'What the hell have you done to yourself?' Stella said.

'You look like a convict,' Sandy said.

'You can't go out in public like that!' Stella sounded horrified. 'People will think we have lice or – or that we're a sanctuary for lunatics. Sometimes I think we are.'

The sympathy I had been feeling for her shrivelled up.

Catherine bit her lip. 'It was my fault,' she said. 'I cut her hair.'

'I asked her to,' I said.

'It's not her fault. I persuaded her,' Catherine said.

'You sound like two silly little girls in some ridiculous school story, playing the heroine,' Stella snapped. 'Come here.' She took my shoulders and spun me round to look at the back of my head.

Sandy gave a low whistle. 'Oh, Catherine! I don't think hairdressing is your forte.'

'Nothing's my forte.' Catherine sounded close to tears but I was the one with something to cry about.

I ran my hand up the back of my head. It felt like our old shoe-brush at home. I had a rush of homesickness, thinking of Leo, before he went to France, cleaning the family shoes on a Saturday night for Mass on Sunday. His and Dad's shiny brogues, Mammy's good buttoned shoes that I used to try on when she wasn't looking, and my own favourites with the silver buckles, that I'd insisted on squeezing my feet into long after I'd outgrown them. Daddy would have been at Mass alone today, and his shoes mightn't have been polished. I was the only one who did it since Mammy died. I scuffed my toes into the grass and felt like a stupid wee girl. *If I'd known what a firebrand she was I wouldn't have had her here.* Well, I might look ridiculous but all the more reason to act with dignity now.

'It's my own fault,' I said. 'I'm sorry if it disgraces Helen's Hope or … or is against its spirit. I won't go out without a hat, you can be sure of that. But please don't punish Catherine.'

Stella ran her hand over the shorn mess that I still hadn't seen and that, in my imagination, was getting uglier and uglier. My nerve-endings shivered at the touch of her fingers. 'You'd better get it tidied up.' She glanced at Sandy. 'Any good at barbering? If Cassie or Scottie sees her like that they'll have fifty canaries apiece. There'll be wigs on the green. Literally.' She glanced down at my discarded hair lying on the grass.

Catherine bit off a giggle.

'Funnily enough, barbering isn't one of my many skills,' Sandy said. But then he added, 'It's one of Edith's though.'

'Edith?'

'She always cut her brother's hair before he died. I'm sure she'd help. I'd go and fetch her only I promised Mother I'd be back for afternoon tea. Helen's parents are coming. I'm late as it is.'

'I'll go.' Stella turned to us. 'Can I trust you not to get into mischief when I'm gone? I don't want to come back and find the house burnt down or a riot in the garden.'

'Promise.'

When they had gone Catherine and I both collapsed on to the grass.

'Phew!' Catherine said. 'I knew Stella could be a bossy-boots but I've never seen her so cross. And, oh, Polly! I'm so sorry.' She put her hand in her skirt pocket and took out the small hand-mirror that normally lived on her bedside table. 'But Edith's bound to work magic,' she said. 'Look how nice her own hair always is.'

'I might need more than magic.' I held out my hand for the mirror. And gasped. My eyes filled with tears. I'd never been pretty, not like Flora or Stella or Catherine herself, but at least I hadn't looked like a freak. Now my eyes looked huge – the fact they were rounded in horror didn't help – and my hair stuck out in odd tufts.

'It's not as bad at the back.' Catherine pulled out my own mirror and held it at the back of my head so I could see. I bit my lip. It was neater than the front but still didn't look like normal hair on a normal person, certainly not on a girl. I felt like bursting into tears, but Stella and Edith appeared just then so I made myself take a deep steadying breath.

'I ran into Edith on her way here, as it happens. She'll sort you out now. Catherine, Cassie's ready to see you. If I were you I'd go and tidy myself up first.'

Edith whistled when she saw my hair. 'Oh dear,' she said. 'But it'll grow back.'

'In about a million years,' I said.

'Don't be daft. Boyish crops are all the rage. And you can grow it into a bob like Stella's if you fancy it.' She grinned at Stella, who didn't look remotely pleased at the idea of me looking like her in any way. Not that I ever could. Edith fingered her own soft brown hair which was plaited round her head today in a kind of coronet. 'Honestly, I envy you. Mine gets so heavy on days like this. Maybe I'll go for the chop too.'

'Don't you dare!' Sandy appeared behind them. 'Your hair's your crowning glory.'

'Thought you were in a rush?' Stella asked.

'I know, but I heard Edith's voice and...' He smiled at Edith in a soppy way and I saw Stella's lips harden. Sandy and Edith wouldn't have noticed; they clearly could see only each other. 'Do you want to come for a walk along the towpath later? It's a lovely day.'

Edith beamed and they made arrangements. Stella's lips didn't soften, and my sympathy for her blossomed again: I knew how it felt to be jealous.

When Sandy had left, Edith looked at Stella. 'Can you put up with me for a bit after I sort out Polly? I came here for company. Daddy's in one of his gloomy moods and I had to escape.'

'Of course.' She sounded almost hearty. 'You can help me draft my letter to the local UVF. You're more diplomatic than I am. I'm likely to tell them where to stick their flags.'

'Tempting,' Edith said, 'but probably not wise. They've got a fair bit of influence round here.'

I remembered Fraser. *Too good to make our flags? We'll see about that.* And the back of my neck shivered in a way that was nothing to do with the lack of hair.

Edith's hands were steady and sure and I felt myself relax and trust her.

'You're very good at that,' Stella said. 'Sandy says you cut your brother's hair?'

'Yes.' She sounded sad. 'Gilbert was invalided out of the army with rheumatism. It doesn't sound bad, does it, but he suffered terribly. You couldn't see anything. I think in a strange way it would have been easier if he'd lost a limb or something. Then people would have understood.'

'What happened to him?' I asked.

'He died of the Spanish flu,' Edith said sadly. 'He didn't have the strength to fight it, but in some ways he'd sort of died already. I mean the Gilbert who came back wasn't the Gilbert who went away. He couldn't seem to shake off the war, couldn't sort of draw a line under it and move on.'

I shivered. I knew exactly what she meant. But I couldn't talk about Leo, not now, not ever. Instead I said, 'My mammy died of that flu too.'

'And mine,' Stella said. 'See what a lot we have in common, we three?'

Unexpectedly she patted my shoulder and, despite the fact that I looked like a freak and was about to have an almighty row for brawling in the street, I felt suddenly much better.

106

Chapter 17

'TO what do we owe the new coiffure?' Cassie sounded amused rather than cross. Maybe there wouldn't be wigs on the green – at least, not about my hair.

I ran my hand self-consciously over the back of my head. I was going to be doing that a lot over the next few days. 'It was a nuisance. It got in the way of the sewing machine. It's not against the rules, is it?'

'No.' Her tone hardened. 'But brawling in the street is.'

I looked down at the parquet floor.

'I appreciate that you were provoked,' Cassie went on. 'And I'm not condoning what those boys did. But we can't have Helen's Hope girls behaving like guttersnipes.'

I stared at my shoes and thought that it was less than a week since I had first been in this office, promising Cassie how good I would be and how she would never regret having me at Helen's Hope.

'We are the objects of … curiosity, locally.' Cassie sighed and pinched the skin between her brows the way Mammy used to do when she had a headache. 'Even before the present troubles, some people were suspicious of us.

People who don't think Catholics and Protestants should live together, and moreover don't like the idea of women living independently of men.'

'I know,' I said. 'Stella's always saying that. And I'm really sorry. But they were horrible. They said disgusting things about Catherine.'

'I understand.' She leaned forward, resting her chin on her hand, and looked friendlier. 'When I was your age I was a suffragette. I went to rallies, carried banners, interrupted public meetings shouting out "Votes for Women". I was called all sorts of things. A hoyden, a disgrace to womanhood. I was told I'd never find a husband – well, that was true!' She smiled, as if she didn't mind that at all. 'So I know what it's like to be abused in the street, but –'

'We were only walking home from Mass!' It sounded like the younger Cassie had gone *looking* for trouble.

'I know. And anyone who thinks that is punishable in any way is deplorable. But, Polly, you have to rise above it. Things in this city are so tense right now. The election is only two days away. You read the newspapers, don't you?'

'Sort of.' All three local papers – *The Belfast Telegraph*, *The News Letter* and *The Irish News* – were set out in the common room every day and we were meant to keep ourselves abreast of current affairs, but only people like Stella and Brigid and Maggie could be bothered. I didn't want to think about it. I certainly didn't want to think about the border slicing through the country round Mullankeen, slashing and dividing. *Ill-divid*, I thought idly.

'You might think it hasn't much to do with you,' Cassie said. 'It's easy to ignore these big questions. But there's nothing good about being ignorant. Helen's Hope is meant to be a community where you young women learn from each other. I spent most of my life teaching girls – and boys – to read Shakespeare and Chaucer and Keats, and parse sentences and write neat, well-spelt compositions. And these are useful enough things. But I'd rather teach you to think.'

I nodded, hoping this was the right response.

'I'm told you applied yourself well in the factory this week,' Cassie went on, 'and that you've settled down among the girls and take your turn at household chores willingly and competently.'

'I'm used to cleaning.' And I didn't mind doing it in Helen's Hope because we all shared it.

'So I don't propose to punish you. But, Polly, you must make yourself better informed about the issues of the day.' She made a note on the pad on her desk and looked up again. 'You're very protective of Catherine.'

'I always have been.'

'And that's admirable. But one of the skills you girls need to learn is self-reliance. Catherine needs it more than most. Make sure you don't fight all her battles for her. Who else have you made friends with?'

It was hard to think. 'Tessa, I suppose,' I said uncertainly. 'She's great fun.' But she was more Catherine's friend. They'd bought matching bracelets during the week, pretty blue glass ones. I had pretended not to mind.

'Hmm,' Cassie said. 'She's a lively girl. But don't forget to appreciate the less obvious charms of some of our quieter girls.'

I thought she meant Ivy, who wasn't exactly quiet but whose charms were certainly not obvious, though she had been leaving Catherine more or less alone lately, but Cassie went on to say, 'Maggie is a dear reliable girl. Very sensible.'

'Oh, I like Maggie,' I said. 'She's been very helpful.'

'She would be. She's exactly the kind of girl Helen's Hope was set up for. We have great hopes for Maggie.'

I wondered if these hopes would involve Maggie having to go away to take a good job. I hoped not. Cassie picked up some papers, my signal that the interview was over.

'I promise I'll try to … er … respect the spirit of Helen's Hope,' I said.

'That's all we ask. Maybe things will calm down in the city. And in the country.' But she didn't sound hopeful.

Chapter 18

THE whole city seemed to squirm with unease. The election took place on the Tuesday and everyone expected trouble.

Cassie went to vote straight after breakfast, looking stern and important. 'This will be you one day, girls,' she said before she left. 'I hope you'll always remember to do your civic duty. Remember the women who fought and died for your right to do so.'

Stella looked fierce. Girls like Brigid and Maggie looked serious. I remembered what Cassie had told me on Sunday about her suffragette past, and I'd heard that Stella's mother had been a passionate suffragette too.

'Is Scottie not going to vote?' I asked Maggie.

'She's not eligible,' Maggie said. 'She's not a householder. Isn't it ridiculous! If she were married to a man who was a householder she could vote, but because she lives here with Cassie she can't.'

'That's not fair,' I said.

I was glad not to have to go out into the streets that day. Tessa came home from the lemonade factory full of tales of gangs loitering outside polling stations, intimidating voters.

Catherine said, 'I won't be brave enough to vote when I am old enough. And I wouldn't know who to vote for.'

'All the more reason to be well-informed,' Maggie said.

'Och, everything will be grand and peaceful by then,' Tessa said at the same time.

I didn't see how.

THE unionists won a massive victory. Ivy went around grinning and I heard her humming 'God Save the King' in front of the Catholic girls one wet evening when most of us were crammed into the common room, reading or chatting.

Unluckily for her, Stella heard too.

'Shut up, Ivy,' she said. Stella's voice was loud and clear and everyone stopped and listened.

Ivy tossed her head. 'I'm only singing the national anthem of this country. You may not like it, but there's been a massive unionist majority. Ulster has spoken. Ulster's British. Anyone who can't accept that can go and live over the border with their own kind.'

She said it as if the border were a fixed and easy thing, just something you could hop over into a different world. A line you crossed once and that was that. I thought of the way the fields and roads meandered around Mullankeen; how you could go from Armagh to Monaghan and even into County Louth and back again without going more than a mile or two or even noticing. How Daddy had said the border was only a temporary solution. Ivy hadn't a clue.

'And anyone who doesn't like the values of Helen's Hope can go and live somewhere else too,' Stella said.

Ivy muttered, 'I was only humming.'

Nobody was quite sure what to say. I put down *The Irish News* and picked up *The Belfast Telegraph*. Very few girls read both, but I was determined to become less ignorant. It was confusing; they disagreed with each other so I didn't know what was true. While the *Telegraph* was celebrating the result as a victory against IRA murderers and the 'attempt to drive the Union Jack from these shores', *The Irish News* hated the very idea of this new Northern Ireland. It talked about the ridiculousness of a parliament to govern this small corner and said it 'did not indicate an institution that was likely to endure'. Which made everything around us feel fragile and uncertain. And at home in Mullankeen, there was a nationalist majority who said they wouldn't recognise the legitimacy of the new state. I thought of Daddy and Leo and the graffiti on the shop wall. I sort of wanted to be there, to make sure they were all right – well, Daddy, at any rate – but I wanted to be here too, in Helen's Hope.

I sighed and laid the paper down.

'You're no fun since you had your hair cut,' Tessa complained. She was sprawling on a big floor cushion, holding a twirl of her own hair up to the lamplight and searching it for split ends. The light sparked off the blue glass of her bracelet. 'It's like Catherine cut off all the spark.'

'I want to understand what's going on,' I said.

'I suppose Cassie said you had to?'

'She said it would be good for my – what did she call it? – somethingy awareness.'

'But it's so boring.'

'It's important. This is the future of our country.'

Tessa gave an exaggerated sigh and flung her arm over her face. 'You're doomed! Next thing you'll be handing out political tracts outside the Workers' Mission.'

'Hardly.' I laughed. It would be so boring to hand out tracts! And scary too, standing out in public. I might be a firebrand, but I couldn't see myself doing anything like that.

Chapter 19

MAY gave way to June, and the violence in the city intensified. Most days saw stories in the papers about shootings and burnings and people forced out of their homes. A few more country girls left Helen's Hope. Their families didn't want them in the city. Even when it wasn't in the papers, we knew – sometimes you would wake at night and smell the burning on the soft June air and hear the shouts and crashes of riots.

'I wish Mammy would send for me to go home,' Catherine said.

'She won't. Daddy's last letter said there was a lot of trouble around Mullankeen. They think we're better off here than there.'

That wasn't all Daddy had said. For the first time in ages he'd mentioned Leo:

> He's very subdued since you left. He hasn't been going out so much; I think he feels safer at home. He never goes to Fox's now. There's been a lot of IRA shootings in the south, of ex-servicemen. Not round here, Cork and Galway and places like that,

but of course it makes us nervous. He asks after you, dear, and I'm sure he would love to hear from you. He never mentions his unfortunate lapse the day you left, but maybe if you could write and let him know you forgive him ...

I didn't tell Catherine any of this. I felt that she had enough to deal with. Ivy was laying off her since I had come, but she wasn't finding her college work any easier and she was fretful and pale, her nails bitten down. Maggie offered to help with her shorthand, but Catherine said it was bad enough doing it all day without having to do it in the evenings as well. She and Tessa did a lot of giggling in corners.

One hot night I woke from a troubling dream about Mammy and Leo and Stella and Flora's pony – all mixed up – and lay tossing and sweating, listening to Tessa's regular breathing on one side of me and Catherine's snuffles on the other, and, in the distance, the shouts and whoops and crashes that seemed to disturb every night in Belfast. The curtains hadn't been pulled properly and moonlight sliced through the gap between them. Catherine had pushed off her bedclothes and the light lay across her in a silver line from her curls to one pale arm flung across the pillow. She looked angelic. I wondered what she dreamed about. Did she still think about Jamie McMahon or were her nights haunted by shorthand?

I pushed my sheet and blanket off but the room was still stifling. I would open the window, see if the fresh air would help me sleep, hope there would be no trouble tonight. I leaned on the windowsill and undid the catch, before pushing the window open very carefully – it often rattled and I didn't want to wake the others, especially Ivy who was bound to be mean about it. Still, she seemed very deeply asleep, turned away from me in a fat heap of bedclothes. She must be sweltered.

There was a light in the factory. That wasn't like Stella! She was so careful to turn everything off. And Scottie always did her rounds before bed to make sure the house was secure and all the lights were off. Maybe it was a trick of the moonlight? No, it was the yellow of electric light, not the silver of moonlight. Was someone in the factory? Was Stella working late in her office? Or was it something scarier? Burglars?

The girls in stories were never done catching burglars in the middle of the night. I didn't fancy it. I looked at Catherine's face, its anxiety smoothed out by sleep. It would be mean to wake her. And Tessa – Tessa would love catching burglars but –

Maybe she would love it too much? Maybe she would somehow make things worse? Better to wake Cassie or Scottie. What a pity there were no men on the premises overnight. Sandy would have made a much better burglar catcher than any of us. I remembered the way the boys in the street had melted away when he'd appeared.

Sandy! I remembered something else. *We don't get much chance to be alone.* Were Sandy and Edith meeting in the factory at night? Surely not! Edith wasn't that kind of girl. But … I looked at Catherine's sleeping face and remembered how she had blushed when she talked about Jamie. Tessa saying she'd been sent to Helen's Hope to keep her away from unsuitable boys. Maybe anyone would be that kind of girl given someone they really wanted to be with. It was funny that I was the one everyone said would go to the bad and yet the idea of meeting a boy in secret didn't appeal to me in the slightest.

Well, if that's what was going on I certainly wasn't going to tell anyone. I crept back to bed and fell back to sleep to the distant roar of fighting.

Chapter 20

MISS KENNEDY told us she was closing her shop and going to live with her sister on the Falls Road.

'Sure there's more trouble over there than there is here,' Brigid said.

'Och, I know, but I'd be with my own sort,' she said. 'Did you hear the police were called in to protect Catholic workers at Gallaher's and the Orangemen fired at them? It's desperate altogether, so it is.'

The shutters went up on the shop the next day, and within hours someone had scrawled on the bright green paint, GOOD RIDDANCE FENIAN SCUM. We saw it on our way home from Mass, and nobody said anything. My breath caught in my chest, wondering about what had been written on our own shop. Daddy had never told me. When we got home, we found five big jars of sweets in the porch, with a note.

> You girls may as well have these.
> All the best,
> Miss Maria Kennedy

'Butter balls!' Tessa said. 'Yum!'

'And toffees,' Mary said.

'Bagsy me the clove rock!'

'There'll be no bagsying,' Brigid said.

Tessa sighed. 'I suppose that would be against the spirit of Helen's Hope. We'll have to divvy them all out exactly.'

'We can talk about it at the next meeting,' Brigid said.

The meeting didn't start well. Brigid's report about the factory was depressing – no new orders – and led to the usual mutterings from Ivy. The King was coming to open the new parliament, and the streets – some of the streets – would be decked out in union flags and bunting for the occasion.

'It's daft not to make the flags,' Ivy said, and a few others raised their voices in agreement.

'Look,' Stella said. 'We aren't sewing flags. Ever. So stop asking.'

'But –'

'You know what, Ivy?' Stella's voice was dangerously tight. 'The matter is banned from further discussion.'

'What happened to free speech?' Ivy demanded.

'Waste your breath if you like,' Stella said, 'but nobody here's listening.'

'All right, girls,' Cassie said. 'Let's talk about something nicer. Miss Kennedy's parting gift.' There was a chorus of approval. Cassie and Scottie looked at each other. 'Nice to hear you so enthusiastic,' Cassie said. 'We were wondering if we should give the sweets away to someone less fortunate.'

'Does anyone have any ideas?' Stella asked.

There was muttering and a bit of complaining. Big girls as we all were, we'd been looking forward to those sweets. Still, there must be plenty of people in these streets who never got sweets. I thought of the children's voices I heard from behind the garden wall.

I found myself thrusting my hand into the air.

'Polly?' Stella said, in a resigned sort of voice as if I couldn't possibly have a good idea. *She opens her mouth without thinking.*

I stood up. Speaking in front of everyone was surprisingly scary, but Maggie and Catherine were smiling looking at me, which made me braver. 'Um, well, I wondered…' My voice sounded high and thin. 'The problem is,' I said, 'the local community don't really know what we're about.'

'What's that got to do with the sweets?' Ivy asked.

'Let her speak,' Stella said, which gave me more courage, and when I went on I sounded confident.

'They're suspicious. They think we're a coven of witches or wayward girls.'

'The Catholics think we're too British and the Protestants think we're too Irish,' Maggie said, blushing when everyone looked at her. I smiled at her, grateful for her support.

'And maybe we haven't been as open as we should have been,' I went on. 'Think about it: we keep to ourselves; we've a ruddy great wall round the garden. No wonder people think we're a bit strange. I mean, *I* came here not really knowing what it was – I thought it was just an ordinary girls' hostel.'

'Oh, get on with it,' Ivy muttered, making a great show of yawning.

'Miss Kennedy feeling intimidated into leaving is terrible. But if we have a party with the sweets – an open day – and invite the locals, especially the children, they'll see that we're –'

'Mad,' Ivy said. I glowered at her.

'What d'you mean, Ivy?' You could tell Stella was struggling to keep her temper. Two red spots bloomed in her cheeks. 'I think it's a wonderful idea.'

I beamed.

'Sucking up to the locals,' Ivy sneered. 'It's too late! You've offended the only ones who count – the leaders of the community – and they won't stand for –'

'If you mean those thugs who've tried to intimidate us into making their inflammatory –'

'They're not thugs! They represent the majority of decent, loyal people in this country.'

'Do you mean Protestants?' Winifred said.

I joined in. 'Are you saying Catholics aren't decent people?'

'I'm a Protestant,' Maggie said, 'and they don't represent me.' She started talking about the cause of labour being greater than unionism or nationalism – sounding exactly like Stella – and some of the girls clapped but Ivy shouted, 'Call yourself a Protestant? You might as well be a fenian.'

'Girls!' Stella shouted. 'If we squabble among ourselves what hope is there? This open day Polly's thought of should bring us together, not drive us apart.'

'It's a great idea,' Brigid said, and Catherine squeezed my hand and pulled me back down. 'We can have games in the garden for the kiddies and a nice tea. And we could make coloured bunting to brighten the place up.'

Ivy leapt at this. 'Thought you wouldn't make bunting?'

'We won't make red, white and blue bunting,' Brigid said patiently.

'So will this be green, white and gold?' Ivy asked.

'Don't be ridiculous. It can be yellow. The colour of sunshine and hope and –'

'Cowardice.'

A few of the girls made chicken noises and Stella stood up, her cheeks flaming. She looked very tall and very angry, a sort of avenging angel. 'How can we be accused of cowardice? If we were cowards we'd make their bloody flags and bunting, to appease them. Instead we're refusing, and we're throwing open our gates to say, Come and see us. Come and see what we're all about. And to be honest, I'm scared of who might come through that door if we have an open day. I'm scared of some of the stuff that's come over the wall and through the letterbox. But I agree with Polly. I want us to be open to the people around us. So tell me how that's cowardice?'

Silence. Ivy chewed her lips.

Maggie said, 'Stella, what *stuff*?'

'Nothing,' Stella snapped. 'Forget it. Look, we need to vote on this scheme. Who thinks we should have an open day for the local community?'

I glanced round nervously. I told myself it didn't matter if people didn't like my idea. Stella loved it and in a way that mattered most. If we didn't actually have the hard work of organising it, and got to do something easier with the sweets, that might be all to the good.

Maggie and Catherine shot their hands into the air at once. So did Tessa and Brigid, and, more hesitantly, Winifred and Maisie and Agnes, and then a few more. Not everyone. Not Ivy. But enough to make it clear that the party would go ahead. Cassie was smiling at me. I knew I was still on trial and surely this would make her think well of me. I thought about what Cassie had said about contributing to the community. Apart from working hard at the sewing, and keeping out of trouble, and forcing myself to read the papers, I wasn't sure if I'd contributed much at all, but maybe this would be my chance. The open day had to be perfect and I had to do everything I could to make it so.

Chapter 21

THAT'S how I found myself, a couple of days later, released from sewing yellow bunting and walking round the streets with an old satchel over my shoulder and Maggie at my side. Stella had typed slips advertising the garden party:

Open day at Helen's Hope.
Saturday 18th June 1921.
Come and join us for a garden party.
Teas. Children's Games. Entertainment.
Everyone welcome!

It felt much grander than my initial idea, seeing the words typed out.

'These must have taken Stella ages,' I said.

'I helped,' Maggie said. 'We made carbon copies of course but we don't have a duplicating machine.'

I couldn't help feeling jealous of Maggie working so closely with Stella. 'I don't know why you didn't just make half a dozen big notices and put them in the shop windows,' I said. 'Much quicker. And we'd be home by now instead of traipsing round the streets in the heat.'

'Stella thought it would be friendlier to have invitations through people's letterboxes,' Maggie said.

'D'you think anyone will come? What if it's a disaster? I'd feel such an eejit.'

'There's not much else going on. At least, nothing festive. People love a free tea. And a nosy.'

'Ivy says –'

'Och, Ivy's an eejit.'

Most of the houses were terraced two-up-two-down, with the odd short stretch of three-storey houses. Some were shabby and tired looking, others had freshly blacked steps and shining door-knockers. In some streets the doors opened straight on to the street, and some of the doors were open, children hanging round playing hopscotch or marleys, women sitting on their doorsteps chatting. They weren't only gossiping though: one was shelling peas into a bowl, one was darning socks and one was knitting something grey. They all looked up when they saw us. There was no chance of just posting the invitations through the letterboxes and moving on.

The first woman shook her head when I tried to hand her a slip. 'I don't need tracts,' she said. 'I'm saved. I go to the gospel hall.'

Maggie said, 'It's not a tract, Madam. It's an invitation to a garden party.'

'Garden party?' She looked round the street: all red brick and grey cobbles, not a blade of grass anywhere. The brick glowed in the sun and reflected slickly in the oily puddles by the kerbs that never seemed to dry up though it hadn't rained for a day or so.

'At Helen's Hope,' I said. 'You know, the girls' hostel?'

'That place.' She sniffed.

'You'd be very welcome.'

'Aye, well,' the woman said. 'I'll have to ask my Hubert.' Her tone made it very clear what she thought her Hubert would say.

'Oh, dear,' I said as we walked on, 'I'm sure she thinks we're no better than we should be.'

'Well, look at us,' Maggie said. 'Shingled hair and short skirts. Too modern for words.'

'My skirt's short because I've outgrown it,' I said. I seemed to have grown since I had come to the city, and I was nervous about asking Daddy for anything. 'Not because of fashion.' I was glad she'd described my hair as shingled rather than simply shorn.

'Me too,' Maggie said, 'but try explaining that to my Hubert.' We both laughed. 'I'm never going to ask a man for permission to do anything,' Maggie went on, her voice serious and fierce.

'Me neither.'

At this time of day the streets belonged to women and children. The men were at work, at the shipyard or the rope works or one of the smaller factories. We gave out some slips to a group of girls skipping and a couple of women leaning on their doorjambs in the sun. One of them shook her head. 'No good to me,' she said. 'I can't read.'

Maggie explained what it was, and said she'd be very welcome, and the woman asked about her seven children, and Maggie said they'd be welcome too, and the woman said, well, she supposed it might make a wee change.

At the Presbyterian manse, one of the few big houses apart from Helen's Hope, the Reverend Hamill was coming down his path.

'Dare you give him a slip,' Maggie said, so I waylaid him with my politest simper. He said that was lovely and he would tell his wife.

'And your children,' Maggie said.

On the main road a man was selling matches, or at least a tray of them hung round his neck. He was looking down at the pavement and didn't notice us, but his lips moved as if he was talking to someone. He had only one arm. He must have been the soldier I had heard Sandy tell Stella about, who had come home from the war to a community that shunned him. Like Leo. But he wasn't as lucky as Leo, who came home without a scratch to a family who only wanted to help him, who did everything for him. *Maybe if you could write and let him know you forgive him…* I brushed the memory of Daddy's words away. This man's clothes were shabby and hung from his frame like he was a scarecrow. I closed my eyes and tried to dredge up the name I had heard Sandy use but I couldn't remember it.

'Let's give him a leaflet,' I said. 'He might be glad of the free tea.'

'He looks deranged,' Maggie whispered.

'God love him. It'd be in the spirit of Helen's Hope.'

Maggie shook her head. 'I don't know. There was a man like that in our street. He went off his head one night and attacked his wife with a breadknife. He's in the mental now.'

I shuddered. Remembered Leo's fist looming. The stink of alcohol. But this man was not Leo. Maybe if I could be kind to him, I would get rid of that looming fist in my mind.

'Well, I'm going to. He looks lonely. And sad.' And before Maggie could argue I walked up to him. He jumped and thrust his one hand over his tray as if I was going to steal his matches or something, but then, when he saw me properly, his face relaxed, maybe because he could see I was only a girl.

'Sorry,' I said. 'I haven't come to buy matches. I've no money with me and I've no need for matches. But you might like to come to this.' I thrust a leaflet at him and sped back to Maggie; for some reason I was trembling. I didn't look back to see how he reacted.

'He won't come,' I said, 'but he might be glad to be asked.' I didn't want to say what I knew about him; it would be hard to without admitting that I'd eavesdropped on Stella and Sandy. And without mentioning Leo.

As we turned into the last street before home there was a group of men and lads on the corner. They looked like they were waiting for us. One whistled as we approached. Maggie marched past with a confidence I suspected she didn't feel, but my neck prickled and I held my breath.

One of them called over, 'Here, girls, yous not giving us one of your – whatever they are?'

'We're just putting them through letterboxes,' Maggie said.

'So how come I just seen you giving one to our Phemie and her pals? Is it only for wee dolls?'

'No,' Maggie said. 'Everyone's welcome.' But she didn't sound very certain.

'It's more for women and children,' I said.

'We'll make up our own minds about that.'

Another boy stepped forward and my stomach plummeted. Fraser!

'Nobody hands out anything in these streets without my say-so,' he said.

I felt Maggie raise herself up to her full five foot one beside me. *Don't argue!* I willed her. I scrabbled in my satchel for a slip, but didn't look up, didn't meet Fraser's eye. He must not have recognised me with my short hair and I was keen to keep it that way.

Fraser read the slip, then screwed it up and threw it into the gutter. 'You lot! Too high and mighty – or is that too *fenian*? – to sew our flags, and now you expect us to let our kids go and be brainwashed.'

'It's not – it's just …'

Rise above it, Polly!

'There is nothing for you to fear or be suspicious of at Helen's Hope.'

For a moment I was full of pride at being able to do what Cassie had asked so calmly, so confidently. And then I realised it wasn't me who had spoken, but Maggie. She set her shoulders back and smiled round the boys.

'As I said, you'd be very welcome, though obviously not with that attitude. Good day, gentlemen. Polly, come on.'

She scooped her arm into mine and more or less dragged me down the street. When we were out of earshot she said, 'Phew!' and flapped her hand.

'You were magnificent,' I said. 'I thought I would explode.'

'Exploding doesn't do any good. There's enough people in this city ready to explode.' And though the sun was warm, we both shivered.

Chapter 22

APART from the yellow bunting, which was costing money rather than making any, there was no work for the factory. Sometimes I thought Stella wished I hadn't thought of the open day: she was going round with a clipboard looking stressed and flushed.

'I shouldn't have put "Entertainment" on the invitations,' she said at the next meeting. We were all sitting in the garden on mackintosh squares and cushions and a motley assortment of old deckchairs.

'They won't expect much,' Brigid said. 'I can play the piano.'

'Not in the garden. And Cassie's said we're not to have people in the house.'

'If we leave the window open they'll hear. I don't mind them not seeing me.'

'I can do a Scottish dance,' Maggie said unexpectedly, and Winifred and Mary said they could dance Irish jigs. Edith could play her violin.

'You can play the penny whistle, can't you, Ivy?' Cassie asked.

'I'll play for the Scottish dance but not the Irish one,' Ivy said.

'Don't be ridiculous,' Stella snapped. 'You'll do both or neither. This is meant to bring us together. Surely we can celebrate everyone's heritage?'

Ivy humped a shoulder and muttered about being silenced and oppressed.

'I can play the flute,' Tessa said. 'I'll play anything. A good tune's a good tune.'

'I didn't know you played the flute.' I had shared a room with Tessa for weeks without once hearing her practise any music, though she was often whistling and singing.

'I don't actually have one,' she admitted. 'I used to play my brother's. But he was blinded in the war and it's one of the few things he can still do, so I can't ask him to send it to me.'

'If you play the flute you could play a penny whistle,' Stella said. 'You could buy one for a shilling or two.'

'It ought to be for a penny,' I said, but nobody laughed.

'I'd rather have a flute.' Tessa sounded determined. I wondered if she wanted to go one better than Ivy. 'Maybe I could borrow one?' She looked hopefully round but everyone shook their heads.

'There's a flute band attached to the Orange Hall,' Cassie said. 'I wonder if they might lend –'

'They wouldn't,' Stella said.

'Is there anyone else local we could ask?' Scottie said. She didn't often speak at meetings except about domestic matters, but she always sat beside Cassie and you could see the support coming from her even when she wasn't saying much. She would put her hand on Cassie's arm or smile to show she agreed with her.

Nobody could think of anyone.

'The houses round here might be bursting with unplayed flutes for all we know,' Tessa said. 'If only –'

'But that's just it,' Brigid said. 'We don't know. We don't know because we aren't really part of the community. Ivy's right.' She held her hand up when Stella went to interrupt. 'We're a bit standoffish – or people think we are.'

'That's why we're having this blasted open day in the first place,' I said.

'It was your idea, so I don't know why you're calling it "blasted".'

'I thought this open day would help you work together,' Cassie said quietly. 'Never mind about the flute; Edith's violin will be lovely. Now can anyone volunteer a song? Moore's Melodies? Some Percy French? What about a nice recitation?'

Some of the girls groaned.

'Recitations are so Victorian,' Tessa protested.

Stella said, 'A comic recitation might be just the thing.'

'But nothing controversial,' Scottie said. 'It's too easy to give offence these days. No religion or politics. Something sentimental and silly maybe.'

Tessa clasped her hands in front of her, thrust out her bosom and proclaimed, stretching her eyes and enunciating exaggeratedly:

'Oh, thou demon Drink, thou fell Destroyer;
Thou curse of society and its greatest annoyer.

134

What hast thou done to society? Let me think.
I answer thou hast caused the most of ills, thou
   demon Drink.'

Everyone giggled. But I thought of Leo having one of his spells. The stink of alcohol on his breath. The horrible noises from his room. Once a trail of vomit all down the stairs which I had to scrub away the next morning, my own stomach heaving. The sense that my lovely brother had been possessed by a stranger. The looming fist.

None of it made me want to giggle.

'Polly?' I realised Stella was speaking to me. 'Are you all right?'

'I'm fine,' I said brightly. 'Just can't believe it's really going to happen.'

'It probably won't,' Ivy said sourly. 'Or if it does it'll just be a few nosy parkers and children.'

'Well, that's fine,' Brigid said. 'That's who it's meant for. You didn't think the King was going to drop in, did you?'

Everyone laughed, but I could see Stella look a bit wistful – though I couldn't imagine her actually wanting the King. Still, how wonderful it would be if someone important did show up and see the work we were doing.

Later that day I took one of the printed slips and posted it to the headmistress of Ellis House. She was the only person I could think of. Maybe she would bring some of her girls with her; maybe even Flora would come! I didn't expect it really: there was as much likelihood of the old Leo coming back, but at least I felt I was doing something.

Chapter 23

WE were all meant to be using our particular talents, and mine was cleaning. I couldn't complain when it had all been my idea!

'The factory will be on show,' Cassie said. 'We don't want people traipsing into the house so we'll have to use it for displays. And teas if it rains.'

'It's not allowed to rain.' Stella frowned at her clipboard as if she had written down 'Sunshine on 18th June'.

'But we can be prepared.'

Sandy moved all the machines into Stella's little office on Friday, which left the workbenches free for displays of our sewing and to lay out cups and saucers for teas. (We were borrowing from everyone Cassie could think of – Sandy's family and Edith's as well as hers and Scottie's.) Some girls were baking in the kitchen under Scottie's supervision and with the kitchen and factory doors open I could hear their giggles and Scottie's voice giving orders. Tessa had indeed managed to procure a penny whistle from somewhere and was practising in the back parlour, so the sound of jigs and reels and hornpipes danced in the air. It reminded me of *céilí*s around Mullankeen. Leo used to let me be his partner even when I was so small he had to dance all stooped over.

'They're having more fun than us,' I said to Maggie, who was on her hands and knees, going into the corners and even under the benches with a dustpan and brush. The factory was kept clean, but it was surprising how much dust and bits of thread and fluff could accumulate.

'Och, it's not that bad.' She crawled out from under a bench and straightened her back. She had tied a jaunty pink scarf round her head and had a smudge of dirt on her cheek. She grinned. 'Many's the time I've cleaned up after all our ones, when Mammy's been busy with babies.'

'I kept house since my mammy died,' I said. 'Daddy has a woman from the town coming out now to keep the place clean and make him his tea.'

'He must miss you, being all on his own.'

'He's got my brother,' I said. 'But he's not much company.' It was the most I had ever said about Leo.

Maggie gave me a quick look. 'Are you homesick?' she asked.

I shook my head. 'No. Home – since Mammy died – well …' I frowned and changed the subject. 'And it's such a small town. I was always in trouble.'

'Who with?'

'The nuns, mostly. At school. They were demons.'

'I've never even seen a nun,' Maggie said. '*It is obvious that our social spheres have been widely different.* That's Oscar Wilde,' she said hurriedly. 'Not me. I mean, I'm not saying anything against nuns.'

I shrugged. 'Wouldn't bother me if you did. All the ones I knew were divils.' I put on Sister Mary Aloysius's voice. '"Polly McCabe, you are an affront to Catholic girlhood. Tidy that hair. Fix those stockings. Holy Mother of God, pray for this sinful child." Ugh.'

Maggie looked sympathetic.

'They were always predicting I would go to the bad.' I had a sudden memory of running home from school crying when I was about eight, in trouble for something, and Leo ruffling my hair and letting me play on the swing he'd made over the stream. That was when he'd said I was just spirited. I wondered what had happened to that laughing boy. And that little girl, so easily cheered up.

'Would they approve of Helen's Hope?' Maggie asked, bending down to brush again. She sneezed as the dust huffed round her.

I leaned on my own brush. 'They'd like the usefulness of it – you know, how we all work hard. And it's a community of women which I suppose they must like or they wouldn't be nuns. But they wouldn't like us all mixed up together – Catholics and Protestants. Infecting each other.'

'Did they hate Protestants then?'

'More a kind of pity – you know, poor Protestants. Like the heathen. Not knowing any better.'

Maggie laughed. 'That's exactly the way our minister is about Catholics – he's always getting us to pray for them to see the light. I'd never met a Catholic till I came here.'

'That dustpan's going to overflow.'

Maggie emptied the pan into the sack we'd brought in for the purpose and looked round the big room in satisfaction. 'I'll just go and brush the floor in Stella's office.'

We weren't normally allowed in Stella's office, so I looked round with great interest. There was a desk, with two wicker trays brimful of papers. I saw a letter with the letterhead *Ellis House*, but I didn't like to snoop. There was also an old mug full of pens and Stella's typewriter under a cover. A mahogany filing cabinet stood behind the desk, and there was a photo on the wall of Helen's Hope the day it opened, with a crowd of girls grinning on the front steps. I recognised Stella, of course, and Brigid, and one or two others, and Cassie and Scottie stood at the front door, holding between them a banner which said *Helen's Hope – For a Better Ireland*. The hostel had only been founded in 1919 but somehow the photo looked as if it came from a different time.

The six bulky sewing machines, which had been moved in from the factory, sat against the back wall of the office, which didn't leave much floor space, but I brushed what there was and ran a damp cloth over all the surfaces.

'Polly!' Maggie called. 'Tea break!'

I went back into the main room and found Ivy standing with two mugs of tea. 'Here.' She handed one to me, and a slightly burnt ginger biscuit.

'Some of the bikkies caught,' she said, 'so we're having them.' She looked round the factory. 'Where's the machines?' she demanded. She sounded anxious, even scared, as if they'd been spirited away.

'Stella's office.'

139

'Why?'

'We're setting the teas out in here,' Maggie said.

'Well, they'd better be moved back as soon as this stupid thing is over,' she said.

I shrugged and bit into my biscuit. 'Ugh! This tastes like sawdust, it's so dry.'

Ivy looked offended, so I guessed she had helped bake them. 'The next batch are better,' she said.

'You should get Catherine to bake stuff for the open day,' I said.

'*Catherine?*' Ivy screwed up her face.

'She bakes like an angel,' I said.

Ivy looked disbelieving. 'Never mind that,' she said. 'When are the machines getting moved back in?'

'I don't know. Who cares? It's not like we're overburdened with orders,' I said.

'Well, we know whose fault that is.' Ivy turned tail and stalked out of the storeroom.

ON the morning of the party, Scottie sent me to the dairy for extra milk.

'There's no knowing how many will turn up,' she said, 'but we'll be the worst in the world if we can't give everybody a cuppa. Take someone to help you carry it back.'

'I'll go,' Catherine offered.

'Go on ahead, you deserve a break. You've been a lifesaver with the baking,' Cassie said, and Catherine beamed. Since she'd been drafted in to help with the baking, which soon developed into being in charge, she had grown a hundred times more confident.

The dairy was a couple of streets away, across the main road. Some old election posters were still tied to lamp posts. There were pictures of the King now too – his visit was only a few days away. And lots of flags.

'Do you worry about what's going to happen?' I asked Catherine on the way home. 'I mean with us living on the border.'

'Och, that silly old border'll never last,' Catherine said. 'Nobody at home wants it. Jamie said …' She shook her head. 'Come on – let's hurry so we can look at the frocks in McCutcheon's on the way past.' And I knew that was all she'd say.

'We can't! We need to go straight home with the milk. If it turns we'll be murdered!'

'On the way past. We don't need to stop.'

'I know you when you're looking at frocks. You won't be able to resist.'

But the frocks in McCutcheon's window were very resistible.

'Look at that,' Catherine said in disgust. 'It's like something you'd wear to a funeral. That must be where Edith buys her clothes.'

We both giggled. It was true: Edith favoured dark, sober frocks, not like Stella, who loved bright colours and new styles.

'But then,' Catherine went on mournfully, 'Edith is clever.' She frowned at herself in the shop window. 'Not like me.'

'You're pretty,' I said. 'Though not when you make that face. I'm neither. *And* you're a genius in the kitchen. The buns and biscuits and scones are going to be wonderful because of you.'

Catherine smiled and caught up my arm affectionately. 'You're smart and brave,' she said loyally. 'And you look grand. Your hair's much better like that. Very modish. Thank goodness Edith rescued you.' Then her tone changed. 'Isn't that Ivy? On that doorstep?'

It was. I recognised her rust-coloured skirt. 'What's she doing there?'

'Talking to someone.'

We positioned ourselves so we could see better. It wasn't a house she was standing at; it was a door between two shops, a haberdasher's and a tobacconist's. I supposed it must lead to an upstairs flat or office; it wasn't the kind of door you would normally notice. We saw Ivy nod and gesticulate and then shake her head, as if she was trying to explain something and whoever she was talking to wasn't happy about it. The person stepped forward just far enough to for us to see that it was a man: I caught the glow of a cigarette end at the end of a blue flannel sleeve.

Then the door shut and Ivy stood back from the step. She raised her hand to knock on the door again, and then changed her mind. She shoved her hands in the pockets of her skirt and clumped back down the street towards Helen's Hope.

'She looks down in the mouth.' Catherine said what I was thinking.

'D'you think she's courting and he's thrown her over?'

'Maybe he's found someone nicer. That wouldn't be hard.'

'She doesn't bother you any more, though, does she?'

'No. Not since you came. But I still don't like her.'

'Me neither.' But something about the slump of Ivy's shoulders made me feel sorry for her. I didn't think it was courting – Ivy never showed any interest in anything like that; she was one of the more prudish girls, often turning her nose up when Catherine and Tessa giggled about boys.

Whatever it was, it didn't seem to be making her very happy.

Chapter 24

IT was cool and dim in the kitchen after the bright sunshine outside but you could hear the shouts and laughs of the children. It was so exciting to see this idea I'd had being an actual thing, with real people. Stella and Cassie were making yet another pot of tea. I opened the biscuit tin and emptied the last few dozen ginger biscuits on to a plate.

'The children are going mad for these,' I said.

'The races are tiring them out.' Cassie spooned tea into the biggest pot. 'Oh, Polly, not that plate. It's cracked. We don't want people talking about us!'

'Is it?' I squinted at the willow-pattern plate. I couldn't see a thing wrong with it.

'There, under that flower. You can hardly see it.'

'Oh, yes.' I moved the biscuits on to a different plate.

Cassie looked out the back window and smiled. 'Brigid's very good with them.'

'Naturally bossy,' Stella said. Cassie looked at me and we both laughed, and after a moment Stella laughed too. 'All right,' she said, 'maybe it takes one to know one.'

'But it's going brilliantly,' I said.

'Not if you don't get back out there with these bikkies.'

I went outside. Luckily the weather had obeyed Stella's hopes and the garden was dotted with women sitting at tables in the sun, fanning themselves and gossiping. Some of the tables were only orange boxes with old tablecloths flung over them, but Edith had put a jam-jar of flowers on every one so it looked festive. Ten small children were attempting a three-legged race, each with one leg tied to her neighbour. There was no sign of anyone from Ellis House. That had been a silly idea; I was glad I hadn't told Stella but had just posted the invitation in secret.

I found Maggie, Tessa and Catherine and leaned against the wall with them, watching the children bash into each other and pull each other over. They looked good in their white frocks; Catherine and Tessa had splashed out on big blue velvet bows to tie back their curls, and even Maggie had pulled the fringe of her short hair into a slide. Mine was still too short to prettify.

'You'd think three legs would be better than two,' Tessa said.

'They hold each other back.'

Two determined small girls who had walked the whole way marched through the finishing tape – a skipping rope held by Maisie and Agnes – and everyone else collapsed in heaps.

'Don't stop!' Brigid called. 'There's prizes for second and third too!'

'Rather her than me,' Maggie said. Her eyes narrowed and she pointed at the gate in the back wall, which was open for today. 'What are those men doing here?'

Oh, help, I thought, *I hope the soldier hasn't turned up. Another of my daft ideas.* I couldn't really imagine him in this throng.

'Hardly men,' Catherine said. She sounded disgusted but also nervous. I looked where Maggie was pointing. It was Fraser's henchmen, three of them. But not Fraser. They were looking round, pointing things out and jostling each other.

'Will I get Sandy to throw them out?' Tessa suggested.

'It says everyone welcome on the leaflets,' Maggie said.

'But they're only here to cause trouble.'

'We don't know that,' I said. 'Fraser's not with them.' What would Cassie or Stella do? I remembered Cassie's voice: *Rise above it!* Stella's determination to make today a success. And my promise to keep the spirit of Helen's Hope.

'We'll offer them a cup of tea,' I said, 'the way we would with any other guest.' And with my heart thumping I marched up to the boys, Maggie and Catherine a few steps behind me. Tessa didn't follow.

'You're very welcome,' I said. To my surprise my voice sounded calm. 'Would you like a cup of tea?'

'I'm sure you'd rather have beer,' Catherine said easily, 'but I'm afraid it's all temperance beverages.' She rolled her eyes as if she found it all a bit ridiculous and knew they would too, and then led the way to the factory, her curls bouncing on her shoulders, and they followed like lambs, one of them even taking off his cap and smoothing down his brown hair. I couldn't believe Catherine could sound so confident. Pity she couldn't have some of that confidence at college. Maybe she could go to a domestic

146

science college instead. That would be much more in her line than typing.

Maggie and I stared after them; they hadn't even looked at us. And though that was a relief, it was sort of annoying too.

'It's because she's pretty,' Maggie said matter-of-factly. 'Will we go and clear some dishes, make ourselves useful?'

Before we had the chance, another man appeared in the gateway. Unlike the boys he didn't stroll straight in like he owned the place, but hesitated, eyes darting round the scene. My stomach gave a lurch.

'It's that soldier,' I said, and when Maggie looked blank I added, 'the match-seller. I invited him, remember?'

We went up to the soldier. 'You're very welcome,' I said.

He took off his cap. 'I … I saw the gate open. It says teas.'

I realised he was hungry. And lonely. Selling matches couldn't be much of a living. He looked scruffier than I remembered, his jacket stained and his hair uncombed. One or two of the children giggled and a few of the mothers frowned. I felt the soldier hesitate and boldly took his arm, the way I used to take Leo's a long time ago. I wished he didn't remind me of Leo. I wished he hadn't come. But I'd invited him.

'It certainly does,' I said heartily, 'and we're the very girls to lead you to them. Come with me.' Maggie went on his other side and we escorted him to the factory where Scottie was serving the teas. I made myself chatter as if he were just one of the girls.

'This is where we do our sewing,' I said. 'You wouldn't think it was a factory, would you? These benches normally

147

have sewing machines on them. Do you see the yellow bunting? We made that but we make all sorts of things.' He didn't say anything in reply, clutching his cap in his one hand.

'Would you like to sit at this bench just inside the door?' Maggie suggested. 'It's quiet but you can see everything. What's your name? I'm Maggie and this is Polly.'

'It's Patrick Neill,' he said. 'You can call me Patrick.' Until then, I'd thought of him as a middle-aged man, but now I saw he was probably about Sandy's age, with a thin, anxious face and very blue eyes.

Hardly anyone was taking their tea inside the factory. A middle-aged woman I'd never seen before, in a bright mauve hat with an artificial bird perched on its side, moved her chair along to make room for Patrick.

'Jolly good show,' she said. I didn't know if she meant the factory, or the tea, or the fact that we were obviously helping a lame duck, but I smiled and said, 'Thank you, ma'am,' in my politest voice.

Patrick Neill tucked into the sandwiches Maggie brought like someone who hadn't had a meal recently. His hand shook on the cup but he drank two cups of tea very quickly. Maggie collected some extra sandwiches and biscuits, and some of Miss Kennedy's sweets, and put them in a paper bag.

'If you'd take these home with you,' she said, 'you'd be doing us a favour. We made far too much.'

'Thank you,' he said. 'You're lucky to have a place like this.'

He looked round the factory. Of course it didn't really look like a factory today, with the machines away, just a big room. I remembered Sandy saying he lived in a hostel, but I guessed a men's hostel wouldn't be much like Helen's Hope. His jacket was crumpled and damp, and he didn't smell like someone who had a bathroom. His boots were so worn that one of the soles was flapping. I supposed he did a lot of walking, tramping the streets with his matches. It was quiet in the factory, faint laughter and chatter from the garden drifting through the open door. Maggie and I waited on Patrick as if he were royalty, but it was hard to know what to say; he was so quiet and nervous. I couldn't imagine him in battle.

A bell clanged and Patrick's cup shot out of his hand, splattering a stream of tea over the bench and all over Mauve Hat's skirt. I shot my hand out to catch the cup before it rolled on to the floor.

'I'm so sorry,' he said. 'Oh, dear, what a mess.'

'It's nothing.' I set the cup upright. I remembered Leo sending a cup across the table – but he had been drunk. And he had two perfectly good hands. There was no excuse for *him*.

'Ladies and children – oh, and I see we have a few gentlemen too – the entertainment is starting in five minutes!' Stella's voice rang out almost as loudly as the bell.

'May I take you to clean your skirt?' I asked Mauve Hat quietly, not to cause a fuss.

'It doesn't matter,' she said. 'It's only tea. No harm done.'

Maggie patted Patrick's arm. 'Don't worry. That bell makes *me* jump out of my skin every morning. Or at least out of my bed.'

It was a feeble joke but we were all glad of it, though his hand couldn't seem to stop shaking, and sweat beaded his temples. I remembered Sandy, the night I had arrived here, after the shock of the riot and Stella's injury. He had shaken like that. And Leo. But it was the drink made Leo shake. Wasn't it?

Patrick was staring at the door as if he longed to escape, as if he wasn't quite sure what he was doing here, but politeness marooned him. Or maybe he was too upset to move. I thought of going to fetch Sandy but a burst of piano music told me that the entertainment had started and I couldn't squeeze past people without being rude.

'I have to go and get ready for my Scottish dance,' Maggie said and slipped out.

As Brigid was inside the house with the windows open, her playing wasn't terribly loud, and Patrick seemed to calm down as the melody continued. Maisie and Agnes sang a comic song, and he relaxed enough to smile. Winifred sang 'She Moved through the Fair' unaccompanied, haunting and plaintive, and everyone clapped and clapped and shouted 'More!' and 'Keep her lit!' until, after a slight hesitation, she followed it with a song in Irish, and they clapped that too and some of them said she should be on the stage in the Opera House. Then Brigid came out, blushing when everyone clapped her, and a stocky young man in a shabby tweed jacket went up to her and kissed her cheek. I guessed it was her Martin.

'Now for some Irish dancing,' Stella said.

I couldn't see her face from where I was sitting but I could imagine her looking round challengingly at the word *Irish*, though nobody seemed bothered. The women sat back in their chairs and the children clustered round.

Tessa and Edith came forward, Tessa holding her penny whistle and Edith her fiddle. She tucked it under her chin, nodded at Tessa and they started to play, a jig or a reel, I never knew the difference. Mary and Winifred danced, backs straight, legs flying and their hair, which they had left loose, bouncing. They were both in white frocks, as we all were for the occasion – Daddy had sent my best dress from home – and they looked lovely. All the women clapped and said things like, 'Och, it's pretty, right enough,' and the children clapped their hands to the beat. Mauve Hat was smiling and nodding as if she found it all delightful, the bird on her hat dipping and diving as she kept time with the music. I had no idea who she was – she didn't look or sound local. The Reverend Hamill's wife, maybe.

'Maggie's turn,' I said to Patrick.

Maggie had tied a tartan sash across her chest. She looked odd without her glasses. She said the audience would only be blobs to her but that she would feel less nervous if she couldn't see their faces. The Scottish dance was different from the Irish one mostly in the way she moved her arms, but everyone reacted in just the same pleased sort of way. I found myself smiling at her with a kind of pride, an idiot grin I knew she wouldn't see. I realised she was my first proper friend. Catherine was my cousin and I loved her, but we were friends more because we were family than because we had much in common. And what I'd felt for Flora and still did for Stella – well, that was hero worship, I suppose, a kind of pash on someone a bit glamorous. Quite fun, but not the same as a solid friendship with an equal. I felt a rush of affection for Maggie. She looked so different from her everyday self – lighter and springier, her cheeks pink.

Ivy, who was playing her whistle for the Scottish dance, also looked different from usual, her head swaying in time to the lilting tune, her foot tapping out the beat. Whatever had been bothering her when we'd seen her in the street, she seemed to have forgotten it.

The boys were lingering just outside the factory door. One of them said something about Maggie's legs which made me blush. But the one who had taken his cap off gave him a dunt and said, 'Catch yourself on, Ernie.'

Lots of children clamoured forward asking if they could dance.

'I could teach them something easy,' Brigid said. She said to Tessa, Edith and Ivy, 'Can you play "The Waves of Tory"?'

I remembered Ivy saying she wouldn't play for the Irish dancing, but she seemed to be swept up by the music now and stayed where she was, blowing spit out of her whistle. I saw Cassie and Stella exchange pleased looks. Maybe the spirit of Helen's Hope was working in Ivy at last.

Brigid got eight over-excited children to take partners and form a set. She shouted instructions to them and, though they sometimes went the wrong way and tripped over their feet, they did their best to do what she said. One small girl in a shabby blue frock, pale plaits flying round her like ropes, skipped harder than anyone else and watched Brigid intently to make sure she was doing the right thing. Patrick was watching with a sad look in his eyes, and I wondered if he had little sisters, and if he missed them. Had Leo missed me when he was away at war? He'd never told me so. He'd never acted like it. *He asks after you, dear, and I'm sure he would love to hear from you … if you could write and let him know you forgive him …* I pushed Leo out of my head – I didn't know why he was barging his way in so much today. Mauve Hat, too, seemed fascinated with the little dancers, watching them with her hat bobbing up and down.

'Isn't Brigid brilliant with them?' I heard Cassie say, and Martin, who was leaning against the door of the factory, nodded.

'Aye, she's some girl, Miss Cassidy.' His voice was full of pride.

'I suppose you're going to marry her and take her away from us soon,' Cassie went on.

'Chance'd be a fine thing! Sure I can't get more than a day's work at a time since those bastards drove us out of the yard.'

The bitterness in his voice cut through the sweet lilting ripples of the music. I felt Patrick stiffen beside me, and I was very aware of Fraser's mates not far away. But nothing happened.

The children begged for another dance, but Brigid laughed and said they'd have to get on with the entertainment.

'Can we come here and learn to dance, Miss?' The girl in the shabby blue frock clasped her arms together tightly as if to hold fast to the joy of the dance. Brigid looked at Cassie.

'We don't have the facilities,' Cassie said. 'There's not a room in the house big enough. I'm sorry.' She smiled at the little girl.

'We can dance in the garden,' the little girl said.

'You can't,' Sandy said. 'It'll take the grass months to recover from today.' But he grinned. He was livelier than usual; everyone seemed different from their everyday selves, brighter and sharper.

'And it wouldn't work in the winter, I'm afraid, Queenie,' Brigid said. Fair play to her: she knew the children's names already.

'We could dance in thon big hall beside the butcher's,' Queenie said.

'I don't think the Orange Order would take kindly to Irish dancing in their hall,' Brigid said crisply, and Queenie gaped at her.

'And neither do I.' It was Fraser. I hadn't seen him arrive. He grabbed Queenie's arm and she glared at him with tight fury – or was it fear? Stella exclaimed and made to intervene but before she could Mauve Hat stepped forward and said, 'Let go of that child's arm, you big bully.'

Fraser stared at her, and then round at the crowd. Children leaned against their mothers, or each other. Tessa

154

and Brigid and Edith – all the Helen's Hope girls, really, except Ivy whose face I couldn't read at all – looked at Fraser as if he was a worm. I remembered the way he had looked at me on the way home from Mass, and the horrible things he'd said, and was glad he was getting his comeuppance.

But Fraser wasn't going to back down easily. 'Queenie's my sister,' he said.

'Doesn't give you the right to hurt her,' Sandy said.

'Well said, old chap,' said Mauve Hat.

'Yeah, Fraser, you spoilsport!' Queenie yanked away from him, buoyed up by the crowd's support, and Fraser dropped her arm. She rubbed it hard and went back to her own friends, who all petted her. One of them, a wee thing the size of a button, stuck her tongue out at Fraser. It reminded me of all the times I'd stood up for Catherine.

'You're not coming here doing any fenian dancing,' Fraser said.

'You're not the boss of me! I like fenian dancing!' Queenie shouted.

Fraser looked round the scene in disgust and saw his friends. 'Ernie? Billy? Robbie? What the hell are yous doing here?'

They looked at each other and shuffled. Ernie said, 'We only came in to see what was going on. There's no harm in it.'

'It's only a wee dance,' Ivy said.

'Ivy?' Fraser sounded like he couldn't believe his eyes and ears. He looked at the whistle in her hand as if he could happily bash her over the head with it. 'What the hell are you ...? Have you no ...? After I ...? What about ...?'

'Why don't you pick a sentence and finish it, Fraser?' Stella said in her coolest voice. 'Or is that too advanced for you?'

'I'll finish you, you snotty bitch.'

'Language!' Mauve Hat said.

Beside me Patrick Neill started to shake and mutter and cringe.

'Don't worry,' I said as loudly as I could. 'He's just an eejit throwing his weight around.' I sounded braver than I felt. I wanted Fraser to leave Stella alone. I was furious with him for spoiling the lovely afternoon with his bullying. For calling Stella a bitch. But mostly I wanted to get my own back for the way he'd abused me in the street. For calling me ugly. For looking at me like I had no right to exist.

Fraser let out a roar and went for me with his fist. Like Leo. But I wasn't going to let another man hit me! I ducked and he connected with Patrick, who scrambled to his feet and tried to punch back but overbalanced. The bench was too solid to fall but his chair crashed to the ground and next minute he was on the floor, his arm flung over his head, sobbing.

Leo is having one of his spells. Don't go near him, Polly.

It wasn't Leo. It was Patrick. And I'd invited him here. He needed me to help him.

I backed away.

Edith gave Tessa her fiddle, bent down and put an arm round Patrick's shoulders. 'It's all right,' she said in a soothing voice.

'Would you like to come and see our vegetable garden?' Sandy asked. 'It'll be quiet down there.'

He and Edith helped Patrick up, and, after a moment's hesitation, he let them lead him down the path towards the greenhouse. Mauve Hat bent down and picked something off the ground. It was the bag of food we'd given Patrick. She hurried after them. 'He'll not want to lose this,' she said over her shoulder. 'Poor chap.'

Cassie, small but brave, went up to Fraser and said, 'I'll have to ask you to leave.'

'Aye, Fraser, come on. This is for wee dolls anyway,' Ernie said.

Billy and Robbie looked at each other and slunk off after him too, though Billy looked back and grinned at Catherine.

'Oh, God. I made it worse, didn't I?' I asked Stella, and she didn't deny it or try to make me feel better. 'Edith and Sandy were brilliant with him.' And I was hopeless.

'Edith's brother was in poor shape when he came home from France,' Stella said. She gave no sign of being hurt by the phrase 'Edith and Sandy'. 'She spent years looking after him. And of course Sandy understands better than most. Poor man.'

I didn't know if she meant Sandy or Patrick. My brother had come back from the war too. I ought to be able to understand. But Leo had come back in one piece! Except for having the flu, of course, which he'd given to Mammy.

I wish he'd never come home. I wish he'd died instead of Mammy. He killed her anyway.

For the first time I wondered what that must have been like for Leo. For the first time I wondered if he'd come back in one piece at all, or if I just hadn't noticed the cracks?

'Look, Polly, we need to get this show back on the road.' Stella's voice cut through my thoughts. 'It's gone so well, I'm not having it ruined. Edith was meant to play again now but she's busy. Where's Brigid? Or Tessa? Or even Ivy?' She was casting round for all the musicians.

But there was no point. People were getting up to go, gathering their children, brushing cake crumbs off their skirts. The lovely afternoon, my wonderful scheme, had fallen apart.

Chapter 25

THE garden felt very quiet now, even though most of us were in it, sitting round in tired groups in the cooling evening sun. A torn scrap of yellow bunting fluttered from a tree. The grass was scuffed where the children had danced, and we kept finding discarded cups and half-eaten biscuits and stray sweets.

Had the day been a success or a failure? Lots of local people had come and enjoyed themselves. Stella and Cassie and Brigid – oh, lots of people – had said to me more than once what a great idea it had been. But the music and dancing and chatter and good humour had descended into an ugly brawl.

'I wish Fraser hadn't spoilt it,' Maggie said for about the tenth time. She was pale and her eyes seemed huge behind her spectacles.

'We need to tidy up,' Ivy said and everyone groaned.

'Tomorrow,' Cassie said. 'You've all worked hard enough for one day.'

'We shouldn't work on the Sabbath,' Ivy said.

'Monday then. It's not as if there's any work waiting,' Cassie said.

'But the machines are all stacked in the office; it's not good for them.'

'They'll be fine.'

'I could move them before bed,' Ivy said. 'I wouldn't mind.' She sounded almost feverish.

Cassie laughed. 'Ivy, it took Sandy the best part of a morning to move the machines. You wouldn't be able to move even one.' When Ivy opened her mouth to protest, she said, 'Sandy will do it first thing on Monday.'

'Why not tonight?'

'Because he's not our slave!' Stella said. 'You can't expect him to work on a Saturday night.'

'Anyway, he's gone to the picture house with Edith,' Tessa said. 'To see *Dream Street*.'

Some of the girls made whistling noises and Stella said, 'Girls! Don't be so vulgar,' and they looked surprised because Stella wasn't normally a prude. But I knew that she was moved by a broken heart. Though you wouldn't have known by her face: she looked merely cross. It was Ivy who looked ready to cry. Over where a few sewing machines spent the weekend?

We all went to bed early. Maggie headed up just after tea, admitting she had a headache. In the Lavender Room Catherine looked out the window and sighed. She twirled one of her curls round her finger. 'That Billy's a nice boy,' she said.

'He wasn't so nice when he was ambushing us on the way home from Mass.'

She waved that away. 'Och, that was Fraser.'

'Billy was there.'

Catherine giggled. 'He said I'd lovely hair.'

'Well, so you do,' I said. 'I've told you that often enough.' No doubt Jamie McMahon had said the same. 'And Fraser probably wouldn't have come and spoilt the day if his mates hadn't sneaked in first.'

'*You* spoilt the day, Polly,' Ivy said. 'You and Stella. You shouldn't have spoken to Fraser like that. You don't know…' She shivered in her shabby nightie, though it was warm.

'What?' I demanded, while Catherine asked anxiously, 'What does she not know?'

Ivy shook her head and got into bed. She dug her face into her pillow and pulled her blankets up over her.

'What he's like,' Tessa said. She looked secretive and important, cross-legged on her bed, brushing her dark hair. 'What he can do.'

'He can't do anything,' I said. 'He's just a bully, Tessa. You saw him – picking on his wee sister and on that poor soldier. Nobody was on his side when he made a fuss about the Irish dancing. They thought he was being stupid. Because he was.'

'Ivy says…' She bit her lip, looked at the hump of Ivy under her covers and sighed.

In bed, I remembered how strange Ivy had been about the machines. And that man she had been talking to in the street: had it been Fraser? I closed my eyes and tried to call up the scene in my head. A blue sleeve. A cigarette. Fraser smoked. But then most men and older boys did. He hadn't been wearing a blue jacket but he could have had more than one jacket. Not like Patrick Neill, whose jacket was in tatters. Patrick. Maybe I should write to Leo. And then I caught myself on. Of course I wouldn't!

THIS time I knew what had woken me. Someone had left the window open and it rattled in the breeze, the catch scraping and banging at the frame. Cursing, because I was cosy and tired, I got up to close it. And froze. A light glowed in the factory. Again? Who was it? Sandy and Edith, calling in for a wee court on the way home from the picture house? No – Sandy respected Edith too much. I leaned out the window. A hum vibrated on the night air, a sound I knew very well now – the whirr of a sewing machine.

This was ridiculous. Who would be sewing in the factory at this time of night? Anyway the machines were all stacked in the office. That's why Ivy had been so cross.

Ivy? I turned round to look at her. She was huddled deep under the covers, the way she had been that other night I woke up, and I wondered how she could bear it, because it was a hot night with a promise of thunder. Still, some people did like to be snuggled up. I went closer. Stood over the bed. She wasn't breathing. I pulled back the grey blanket and found, not a sleeping girl, but a winter coat and a pillow, heaped up so that to the casual glance it was as if a person was asleep under the covers. How stupid of me! The girls in stories were always playing this trick so they could sneak off for a midnight feast.

But Ivy wasn't at a midnight feast. She was in the factory. I had no idea why, but I was going to find out. I crept out of the room and onto the landing.

The house felt very dark and quiet. Eerie. I thought of going back to wake Tessa but I wasn't quite sure how much I trusted her. And Catherine would have been too scared. Maggie would have been better – I longed for Maggie's steady good sense – but I knew she wasn't feeling well and it would be selfish to wake her. I crept towards the stairs, praying I wouldn't step on any creaking boards. All the doors on the landing were firmly closed, except the bathroom, where moonlight lit up the black-and-white tiles on the floor. The only other light was from under Stella's door and as I crept past I could hear the small noises of someone moving around. Stella. So she was awake! Would she help me?

Without letting myself think too much, I knocked on her door. I half-thought she would ignore it, but the door opened before I had a chance to gather my thoughts and Stella, still in her white frock, hair tangled as if she'd been raking her fingers through it, stood in the doorway. She looked shocked to see me. And though she dashed her hand across her face she wasn't quick enough to hide the fact that she had been crying.

'Polly! What's up?'

'Something odd in the factory.'

'You'd better come in,' she said. Her room was small and neat, with a bright woollen rug over the bed. She must have been writing: a lamp shone brightly on to the desk, showing a page covered in Stella's bold sloping handwriting. A diary? A letter? I wondered who she was writing to. And why she'd been crying. I told her as quickly as I could about the lights and the noise of sewing and that Ivy wasn't in her bed.

'And she was really funny about the sewing machines being moved back tonight,' I reminded her.

'Maybe she's keen to get something finished.' There was no trace of tears now in her voice or on her face. Had I imagined them? With a deliberate casualness she crossed to the desk, switched off the lamp and turned over the pages she'd been writing on.

'But there's no orders. You know that better than anyone.'

She frowned. 'So she's moonlighting. Doing her own work using our facilities. Not very Helen's Hopeish.'

'Will you come with me or should we get Cassie?'

'We'll go ourselves.' Stella looked determined, as if glad of a distraction.

I felt very much like someone in a book as we crept down the stairs and through the moonlit kitchen, the resourceful new girl following the gallant head girl. And Ivy was the baddie.

As we unlocked the back door and headed across the yard there was a crash of thunder and warm rain battered us so hard that we were soaked in the few seconds it took us to get to the factory door.

Ivy, sewing at the back bench, didn't look like a schoolgirl baddie. She looked like an overworked seamstress. It wouldn't have been easy, dragging that heavy machine back into the factory.

164

The wheel spun so fast I could hardly see it. Ivy's foot trundled like a piston. She was so intent that she didn't notice us. Her face was screwed up in concentration and her hand on the white fabric looked rigid. The needle plunged up and down, in and out, in and out, a greedy diving bird, too close to her fingers. Rain pebbled the skylight above her.

'Ivy!' I said.

She jumped, the needle stopped, the wheel kept spinning for a moment and then whirred slowly to a halt, the fabric ruched.

'Damn!' Ivy said, and her hand flew to her mouth.

'What the hell –?'

I was never sure if it was Ivy or Stella who said this. Stella, I think, because Ivy's hand was in her mouth, blood seeping through her fingers.

Stella said, 'Let me see your hand, Ivy.'

'I have to keep sewing,' Ivy said. 'You don't understand.'

Her feet and hands started going again, the wheel whirring faster than ever. She wasn't like a girl in a school story. She was like a girl in a fairy tale. A girl under a spell or a curse, forced to sew and sew until –

Blood seeped onto the white fabric and still Ivy sewed, her face screwed up in concentration or pain or both.

Stella reached under the table and kicked Ivy's foot off the pedal. Everything juddered to a halt. Ivy screamed. 'Leave me alone, Stella. I have to finish this. I can't stop, I need to finish this tonight.'

'You can't; your hand's a mess. I wonder if we should get Dr Scott.' Stella took Ivy's hand; her long fingers pressed the skin of the bleeding palm together but the blood kept oozing.

'Dr Scott won't come out at two o'clock in the morning for a bit of a cut,' Ivy said.

'Scottie then. She'll know what to do,'

'No!' Ivy snatched her hand back. 'You can't tell her. You can't tell anyone.'

Until then we hadn't looked closely at what she was sewing. It was the back of something – plain cheap backing fabric such as I'd started to attach to the back of my nearly finished quilt. I knew Ivy was poor, and I'd assumed she was secretly making something like my own quilt, put together with scraps. Maybe, unlike me, she hadn't actually asked for the scraps and that was why she was so upset at being found out.

I lifted the fabric and turned it over. It wasn't a patchwork quilt. It was a union flag: red, white and blue. In gold letters was emblazoned across the bottom: *For God and Ulster. No Surrender.*

Ivy looked at us with defiant eyes.

'Who's this for?' Stella asked in a dangerous voice. She seemed to have forgotten her concern for Ivy's hand. 'Ivy? You can tell either me or Cassie. I'll fetch her now if I have to.'

'It's only a flag,' Ivy muttered. 'It's to welcome the King.'

'It's banned in Helen's Hope. You know that. All flags are.' Stella sounded tired. 'Look, I'm not going over all the arguments again. You know the rules.'

'But you're not just making a flag for fun, are you, Ivy?' I asked. 'Or to annoy Stella. I mean, coming out here at night. Working in secret. Who's it for?'

And then I knew.

'Fraser?' I asked. She didn't answer, just bent over, clutching her bloody hand.

'Is it' – I tried to remember what Fraser had said the day he had threatened us all after Mass – 'something to do with his Uncle Alec?'

Ivy's face lifted. Her lips were pale with flakes of dried skin. 'H-how did you know? His Uncle Alec's big in the UVF. Fraser promised him the flag for the King's visit on Wednesday. And I – I promised Fraser.' Her voice was little more than a whisper.

'You'd no business to!'

'Brigid said we needed more orders or the factory couldn't keep going. I told Fraser we could do it, no problem, and then you all turned against me! Made me look stupid. After I'd promised.'

'No, we didn't.' Stella sounded at the end of her patience. 'You put it to the meeting and we said no, it was against the spirit of Helen's Hope. All you had to do was tell him that.' She made it sound easy.

Ivy bent lower over her hand and I guessed she was trying not to cry. Stella didn't understand, but I did. Stella was brave and confident, and kind too, most of the time, but I didn't think she had much imagination. She expected everyone to be as bold as she was. She stalked through life, her shoulders back and her chin tilted and her head high. She didn't know what it was to cringe and fear and worry. But I did. I had done ever since Leo had come home and Mammy had died and the landscape I'd known all my life had been ripped in two.

'Ivy.' My voice was gentle. 'Are you scared of him? Did he threaten you?' Leo's fist, looming towards me.

'No! I wanted to help him. I didn't want to let him down. I'd promised.' She turned her face to us. 'You don't know what people say about us round here! I thought this would be a way to – to make them like us.'

'Don't be daft. You saw what happened today. Lots of people came. They loved us. The children want to come and dance. One of the mothers was asking if we could run a girls' club in the evenings to give girls something to do. They clapped at the Irish dancing. They didn't even mind when Winifred sang "Sliabh na mBan".'

Ivy let out a howl of frustration. 'They aren't the ones you have to worry about!'

'We don't have to worry about anyone,' Stella said. 'We know who we are and what we stand for. The people who came today could see that, except for your precious Fraser. And we are never letting Helen's Hope be used for making flags. I'm not sucking up to people like that – I don't care if they like us or not.' Her cheeks were flushed and her hair and eyes bright; she looked like an Amazonian warrior.

'He promised the flag to his Uncle Alec,' Ivy said, 'and his Uncle Alec is not the kind of person you want to upset. Seriously, Stella, you can say what you like about peace and love and mutual understanding, but this is Belfast. There's a war on.'

On and on. Words and loyalties and anger, stitched into us all for generations. Too tightly to unpick. A pair of scissors lay beside the fabric on the bench. I lifted them.

They were sharp. This was the flag Leo had marched away for. The flag Stella had been hurt for. This was the flag that led to the words of hate on our wall in Mullankeen.

Before the others could ask what I was doing I grabbed the flag and cut into it – *slash slash slash* – until it was a heap of ribbons sloshed all over the bench and floor like the tea Patrick Neill had spilt earlier. So now it didn't matter what the arguments were. There was no flag to fight over.

Chapter 26

IVY collapsed. She went limp and grey–white. Stella, with more speed than gentleness, shoved Ivy's head down between her knees, exactly as the girls in books did. But the girls in books swooned when they had scored the winning goal with a broken ankle, or stopped the runaway train, not at the sight of a destroyed flag. And they didn't struggle to sit up and call their saviours all sorts of terrible names. Together Stella and I dragged her outside where the rain on her face seemed to bring her to her senses, and she started to cry and slumped into Stella's arms.

'Poor old Ivy,' Stella said, more gently than I had heard her speak before.

'You don't understand,' Ivy whispered. All her fight was gone. 'You don't know what they'll do.'

'They won't do anything to you; we won't let them,' Stella said. She stroked Ivy's wet hair back from her forehead. Jealousy kicked me before I could tell it not to be so daft.

'It was me cut the flag. I'll go and tell Fraser – or his Uncle Alec, or anyone you like,' I said, more sturdily than I felt. 'I'll say you defended it with your life. Which you practically did.' I gestured at her hand, which was bleeding all over her frock, the blood mixing with rain.

'We'll get Scottie to put you to bed,' Stella said.

We helped her back to the house. The rain had lessened and the sky was lightening into a bruised patchy dawn. Birds sang from the garden. Stella's hair was turning from silver to gold and the bloodstains on Ivy's frock were brightening to red.

'I've never been up at this time before,' I said.

'I have,' Ivy said weakly. 'I've been sewing that flag every night for the last week. Nobody would help me.'

'Good,' Stella said, as we went through the back door into the kitchen. 'The spirit of Helen's Hope isn't completely dead then.' Ivy sank down into a kitchen chair. 'You two wait here,' Stella went on. 'I'll go and dig Scottie out of bed.'

'And I'll make Ivy some hot, sweet tea,' I said.

As I waited for the kettle to boil, I asked, 'How did you even get in? The factory's always locked at night.'

Ivy looked sheepish. 'I had a key copied.' She reached into her skirt pocket with her good hand and took out a key on a piece of string. I took it and pocketed it, meaning to hand it to Stella to put somewhere safe.

BY ten o'clock the sun was out. As Stella and I turned into the street where Fraser lived, I clutched the awkward bundle of ripped-up flag tighter. It had been my idea to bring it.

'We don't want them to be angry with Ivy,' I pointed out. 'They need to see she did actually make the blasted thing.'

Fraser lived in one of the poorest streets Maggie and I had leafleted last week, a tiny kitchen house opening straight on to the street. But the step was scrubbed, and the net curtain in the single downstairs window, though ragged, was clean.

I thought the woman who answered the door must be Fraser's granny. She had very few teeth, which gave her cheeks a sunken look, and her eyes were more exhausted than Ivy's had been after her nights of sewing. Ivy was tucked up in bed now, with orders from Scottie not to move and not to fret.

'What's he done now?' She looked us up and down. 'Don't tell me he's got one of yous into trouble.'

Stella looked extremely dignified. 'Certainly not.'

It might be the other way round – we who were getting Fraser into trouble – but I didn't think it would be a good idea to say so.

Queenie appeared from behind the woman. 'Ma!' she said. 'It's the lady from the Hope place. I forget its name.' She grinned at us, all gap-toothed perkiness. 'Is it about the dancing?' She was wearing the same shabby blue frock as yesterday.

'Away back in, Queenie,' Mrs Wylie said. 'Never you mind.'

'Aww, Ma.' She looked up at her mother, then dodged past her and across the street. 'I'm calling for Bertha!' she shouted over her shoulder. She stuck out her tongue and laughed. I wondered how long she would keep her spirit. If people were already predicting she would go to the bad.

'Are yous from that place, right enough? With those queer women?' The woman folded her arms across her

172

thin chest. 'That's no way to live, so it's not. Yous'll not get yourselves men that way.'

'I have no interest in men,' Stella said, 'except as fellow humans and comrades.'

'Comrades?' She looked aghast. 'Don't tell me yous are a lot of communists. I heard yous were republicans and dear knows that's bad enough.'

Stella sighed. 'We're neither. We're simply a group of women and girls trying to live a decent life, free from the fetters of both unionism and nationalism. We learn from each other.'

'You'd have seen that if you'd come to our open day yesterday,' I couldn't resist saying, mainly to back up Stella.

'Oh, aye? And where would I get the time for that? You lot have no idea about the real world. Our Queenie was back here last night with her head turned about dancing and girls' clubs and I don't know what else. She's out running the streets now instead of helping me.'

'If we could just speak to your son,' Stella insisted. 'Preferably not out in the street. He's been harassing one of our girls, extorting services under threat, and coercing her into using our premises and facilities for illegal political activities likely to cause a breach of the peace.' She sounded like a policeman. A policewoman. I was very impressed and slightly scared.

Fraser appeared just then, filling the doorway, and he looked very unimpressed and definitely not scared.

'Where's Ivy?' he demanded. 'I told her yesterday I couldn't wait any longer. Here, Ma, away on in.'

To my surprise she obeyed him as if he were the parent and she the child. He looked down at the bundle in my arms and his face cleared.

'Ah! Yous have it. I'll take it on round to Uncle Alec now.'

He reached for the flag, but I held on to it, looking to Stella for help. For all my brave words to Ivy I was quaking.

'Here, give us that,' he said. 'Why did Ivy not come herself?'

'We'd prefer to have this conversation indoors,' Stella said.

I guessed she wanted to avoid the situation where I unfurled a mutilated union flag in the middle of the street.

The door opened on to a small room, with a table and chairs and one hard-backed settee. With the three of us, it felt tiny. There was a scullery beyond and I could hear Fraser's mother busying herself and going in and out to the yard. A pair of pot dogs kept guard over the mantelpiece, just like we had at home, and in between them was a large framed photo of a man in uniform. Two flags, a union flag and an Ulster red hand, were crossed under his face and the slogan:

UVF – FOR GOD AND ULSTER!
BATTLE OF THE SOMME 1916

I guessed this was Fraser's father and that he had died in the war. We had a photo of Mammy in just the same place.

'Before we give you this,' Stella said, 'I have to tell you that Ivy did her best for you. She shouldn't have – she was breaking every rule of Helen's Hope, and –'

'She was glad to help,' Fraser said. 'She's a good loyal Protestant. At least' – he sounded suddenly unsure – 'she was until yous got your claws into her.' He spat into the grate. 'Playing fenian music!'

Stella waved this away. 'Don't be ridiculous. It was a folk tune. It was about the sea. How can that be offensive to anyone? Anyway, that's not the point. The point is you knew Helen's Hope won't touch anything political. We'd already refused your order. Twice. You shouldn't have asked Ivy to do it off her own bat. Were you paying her?'

He shook his head. 'We paid for the fabric. She was happy to do it for the glory of Ulster.'

His eyes slid up to the photo of his father.

'She was scared,' I said. 'She might well believe in the glory of Ulster' – the words sounded strange in my mouth – 'but she was scared of you. Scared of saying no.'

I remembered the frenetic way Ivy had been stitching, the relentless paddling of her foot on the treadle, the way she had collapsed when I had damaged the flag.

'Why, Fraser?' Stella asked in a casual tone. 'What's she got to be scared of?'

Fraser shrugged. 'Maybe I know too much about her.' He looked us both up and down as if we were sides of pork hanging in the butcher's. 'You don't know where all your girls come from, do you? I don't suppose Ivy would want her precious friends to find out where she's been.' Again his finger jabbed for the bundle I was still clutching like an awkward baby. 'The answer is everywhere. With everyone.'

Stella gave him a withering look. 'We're not concerned about that.'

'Well, maybe you should be. Bad enough harbouring fenians without them being a load of hoors. We never wanted a home for wayward girls round here.'

'For the last time, Mr Wylie,' Stella said,' Helen's Hope is not a home for wayward girls. It's a commun –'

'Just give me the flag,' he said. 'My Uncle Alec's waiting on it. And he's not a man to keep waiting.'

He sounded agitated. As if he was as scared of Uncle Alec as Ivy was of him. As I was of Leo and Daddy was of the words on the wall of the shop. And Leo was of – well, I didn't know what Leo was scared of – maybe his memories of the war? Maybe everyone was scared of someone. Or something.

I set the bundle down on the table. 'Ivy did her best,' I said. 'For whatever reason – for God and Ulster, or for you, or out of fear, I don't know. But she did it. She stayed up sewing it for nights and nights. She only didn't finish because we caught her.'

I started to unwrap the flag, very aware as I did so of the smaller, identical flag watching me from the mantelpiece. Fraser's father had died for this flag. For God and Ulster. My own father hated it. Flags like this were hanging from lamp posts in some parts of the country and being burned in other parts. This flag meant colonial oppression, or glory and loyalty, depending on your point of view. But now, as I unfurled it on the un-wiped, crumby table in this tiny east Belfast kitchen house, it was a sad, shattered relic. It looked worse than when I'd bundled it up. The backing had come apart from the red, white and blue front, the golden braid was hanging in tatters. Blood smudged the lettering.

Fraser's mouth fell open. 'What the –?'

'I destroyed it.' I said it as sturdily as I could. 'Nobody else. Just me.'

'Why?'

'It's against the spirit of Helen's Hope,' I said. For the first time I said the words without irony, without sort of mocking them. I meant them.

'My father died for that flag!' Fraser stroked a finger along one of the tattered shreds. I imagined Ivy sewing it, night after night, stitch after stitch. 'He signed the Ulster Covenant in 1912. He joined the UVF to keep Ulster British. There's people round here will have something to say about this.'

'Ulster is still British,' Stella put in. 'So I don't know what you're whingeing about. Didn't your lot sweep the board at the election? Hasn't this tiny country been sliced in two? Isn't the King himself coming to open the Northern Irish parliament in the City Hall? Isn't it going to be' – her voice hardened – 'a Protestant state for Protestant people? So you can dry your eyes about one measly heap of fabric. God knows there's enough of them round the place.' She swept it off the table and it flumped on to the dusty stone-flagged floor.

I felt twisty and confused. *There's people round here will have something to say about this.* If it was only a measly heap of fabric, why did it matter so much that Ivy shouldn't have made it? Might it have been better to have appeased Fraser and Uncle Alec and God knows who else than to have made them this angry? Then I remembered the words on the shop wall, and the men chased out of the shipyard, and Miss Kennedy, and Leo, and Patrick, and Ivy bullying Catherine, and being bullied herself by Fraser. No. I knew. It was never right to give in to intimidation.

Stella was clearly enjoying the fight more than I was. Her nostrils were flared, her chin high; she stood tall in the low room.

Fraser fell to his knees and started to gather up the flag as if it was the body of someone he loved, caressing the fabric, but it was so damaged that it kept slipping out of his arms, and in the end he gave up, straightened up and stood face to face with Stella. They were the same height but he was much stockier.

'What am I going to tell Uncle Alec?' he demanded. 'I promised him a flag worthy of the local UVF. In his brother's – my da's – memory. Do you know how many men round here died at the Somme? And you're cutting their memory to shreds?' His voice cracked with emotion.

'Don't bring the war into it.' Stella sounded disgusted. 'You weren't so respectful to Corporal Patrick Neill yesterday.'

'That crazy bloke?'

Stella widened her eyes at the description. 'Corporal Neill lost his arm at the Somme,' she said. She must have been speaking to Sandy and Edith after they'd taken Patrick away. 'Much good the King's uniform did him.

He probably fought side by side with men from round here. Maybe with your father. He's been spat at and kicked in his own streets too. So if you want to bring the Somme into it, get your facts right. Come on, Polly. We're done here.'

She turned to go. But with one swift movement Fraser barred the door.

'Let us past,' Stella said. 'We've nothing more to say. We only did you the courtesy of calling because Ivy was so worried. I don't know why she's so loyal to you.' She shrugged. 'She should have been more loyal to Helen's Hope but –'

'She's not loyal to me.' He spat the words out. 'I thought she was loyal to Ulster but yous have corrupted her. Helen's bloody Hope! Aye, you're right, she is scared of me. Scared of me telling yous she's a dirty wee hoor. You know she was servicing half the yard before she was fifteen? Oh aye, down the docks selling herself for a shilling a time.' He smirked in triumph. He obviously meant Stella to be shocked. This was his trump card.

But Stella merely sighed and said, 'Mr Wylie, you're clearly a bully. I didn't realise you were so disgusting and disrespectful too. Let us go, please, or we shall scream very loudly, and your mother will come. I'm sure she'll be proud of your treatment of Ivy.'

He laughed dismissively. 'I'm not scared of my ma.'

'You're heart-scared of your Uncle Alec, though, aren't you?' I said.

Fraser said nothing, but a muscle twitched beside his eye.

'Good luck with telling him,' Stella said. 'If you hadn't

been so disgusting about Ivy I might have gone to explain to him that it's not your fault you can't produce the flag you promised him. As it is' – she shrugged – 'do your own dirty work. Now let us go.'

He stepped aside and we left, Stella stalking, me more or less scuttling, though I tried to march like Stella. She walked so fast down the street that I had to skip to keep up with her and that made me feel stupid and childish. She seemed furious, her cheeks flaming and her breath huffing like a prancing pony's. I'd no idea where we were going, or if she was aware that I was still tagging along, but I wasn't going to leave her. The street felt cool and airy after the stale, close air of the wee house, but Stella didn't go straight back to Helen's Hope. She cut through an alleyway and across a long thin street that wound downhill to another main road, one I'd never been on before, with more houses and fewer shops and, all along the far side of the road, a park. Green! Apart from the smallish garden at Helen's Hope I hadn't seen grass or trees for weeks. I didn't know how much I had missed them until I felt my heart flip.

'A park!' I said, and now that the silence was broken I went on, 'Stella, you were really brave.'

'Huh,' she said. 'Standing up to idiots like Fraser Wylie doesn't take much courage.'

'Those lies about Ivy –'

'Don't tell anyone.'

'I didn't believe him!' I reassured her. 'Ivy wouldn't – she's too prim and proper. She's always telling Tessa and Catherine off for being flirtatious around boys.'

Stella didn't respond.

'Where are we going?' I asked.

She sighed. 'To call on Sandy. Tell him what's happened. He's sensible.'

'But why? It's over now. We sorted it out.'

'I don't think it's that simple. I don't think this is over.'

Chapter 27

SANDY lived in a street of tall houses beside the park. There were no flags or election posters in sight, and none of the broken glass and old bottle tops which bloomed in the streets round Helen's Hope, only begonias and violas in neat rows behind privet hedges. Sandy's house had a tiny garden and sparkling lace at every window.

'It's very clean,' I whispered, while we stood on the shining doorstep waiting for someone to answer the doorbell. 'I can't imagine Sandy living here.' Sandy, with his hands mucky from gardening, shabby old corduroys and worn tweed cap.

The door was opened by a sharp-faced middle-aged woman with reddish hair. She was no more welcoming than Mrs Wylie. 'She hates me doing manual work at Helen's Hope,' Sandy had said. This wasn't a street for gardeners and handymen; it was a street where men caught the tram to offices, in bowler hats and pin-striped suits.

'He's out,' Mrs Reid said. 'It is Sunday. Day of rest.' She didn't say 'So you shouldn't be bothering him, you tiresome girl,' but she didn't need to. It was in every tightening of her thin lips, every smoothing of her hands over her black skirt.

'Will he be back soon?'

'I am not my son's keeper.' Mrs Reid sounded as if this was a matter of regret. 'Good day, Stella.'

'Phooey!' As we walked back down the path I let out my breath in what I hoped Stella would find a comical sigh. 'She's not your biggest fan.'

'She's terrified I'll get my claws into Sandy. Ha!' Her voice hardened. 'I can guess where he is. Or at least who he's with.'

'Edith?' I dared to say.

'Edith.' And for the first time since we had set out she sounded, not defiant, not brave, not like a policewoman or an avenging angel or the bold head girl, but like a tired girl who had been up half the night and was Disappointed in Love. I remembered that when I'd knocked on her door last night she had been crying. I'd always admired Stella but now I felt I wanted to look after her. I'd only felt that way about Catherine before. But Catherine didn't need me the way she used to.

I had two shillings in my purse and across the road by the park gates was a tea stall. I felt gritty and cold inside with lack of sleep and I bet Stella did too.

'Why don't we go and have a cup of tea in the park?' I suggested. 'The cup that cheers but does not inebriate.' I remembered Catherine joking with the boys yesterday about temperance beverages.

'Why not?' Stella said. 'We've earned it.'

There was a queue at the tea stall. Stella groaned when she saw it.

'You go and sit down,' I suggested. 'You look tired. I don't mind queuing.'

She hesitated. 'Well, if you don't mind.'

'Course not.'

I felt like a new and better Polly as I stood in line, jingling my money in my little leather purse. Stella had walked to a bench almost out of sight, under a tree. I paid for two teas and a bag of buns – I thought I could share them with Catherine and Maggie – and walked carefully towards Stella, a cup in each hand and the paper bag clamped between my teeth. There was a man ahead of me, swaying as he walked, drunk, I assumed, his jacket stained and wet, his boot soles flapping. I sped up to overtake him, balancing the cups carefully, but then he stumbled, and lurched sideways against a tree, and didn't put his hand out to save himself, so he fell. Sprawled on the ground, he made no effort to get up.

A respectable-looking woman pulled her children past and tutted, 'On a Sunday!'

It was Patrick Neill, and if he had looked rough yesterday he looked a hundred times worse today. Yesterday I had frozen, failed to help him. Today I had to do better.

'Patrick!' I set my cups down on the ground. 'Are you all right?' I reached a hand down to help him up, but he looked at me without recognition. 'It's Polly,' I said. 'From Helen's Hope. Where you were yesterday.'

'Oh, aye.' He made no effort to take my hand. He just shook his head. 'They took my matches,' he said. 'And they threw me out.'

I hunkered down beside him. He didn't smell of drink, just of dirt and destitution and despair.

'Who's "they"?'

He shook his head again. 'They threw me out.'

'Of your hostel?'

He leaned back against the tree and closed his eyes. 'Sure what does it matter?' he said.

I had no answer, except, 'Would you like a cup of tea?'

'Is that all you ever do?' he asked. 'Give people tea?' But he took the cup I handed him, though he didn't drink. He was shivering. I put a timid hand on his jacket sleeve and found that it was sodden. I remembered the rain of the night before.

'Do you have nowhere to sleep?' I asked.

He shook his head. 'They took my matches,' he said. He seized my hand, and his hand burned, as if with fever. Stella, I thought, Stella will know what to do. I looked up to see Stella, just a few benches along. She couldn't see me; she didn't know I was watching, and she looked as defeated as she had been last night, slumped, head bent, exhausted. I couldn't bring her another problem.

I fished in my pocket for the key I hadn't yet given up. I set it down beside Patrick. 'This is a spare key to the building you were in yesterday,' I said. 'It's not exactly comfortable – it's a factory – but it's warm and dry, and nobody's there at night. If you needed somewhere to shelter for a few nights…'

He didn't react. I didn't know if he had heard.

I picked up the other cup. 'I have to go,' I said. 'My friend's waiting. Here.' I took out a bun each for me and Stella and gave him the bag.

Halfway to Stella I turned to see if he had taken the key, or the tea and buns, but he was still sitting the way I'd left him.

Stella and I sat on a bench under a huge oak tree. As she drank her tea I told her I hadn't wanted one. 'You're a good kid, to queue up just for me,' she said. The sun warmed my neck and the scent of lilac tickled my nose. We were only ten minutes' walk from Helen's Hope and it seemed a different city, a much nicer and more peaceful one.

I bit into the sugary warmth of my bun. Like most buns it didn't taste as good as Catherine's but I was glad of it. 'Why didn't Cassie set up Helen's Hope round here?'

'She couldn't afford a rabbit hutch in this area. You pay for the privilege of living somewhere safe and quiet. And though we might not have had the same problems, we'd have had others.'

'What d'you mean?'

'They might not have been so bothered about Catholics and Protestants living together but there'd have been the same nonsense about wayward girls. Maybe even worse. Women can't win.'

I sighed. A bit of Stella's bun crumbled and fell, and two seagulls swooped down and had a squawking mid-air battle over it. I threw down a hunk of my own bun to even the score, but the same gull gobbled it up and the other one flew away empty-beaked.

'Greedy guts,' I said. 'The world's ill-divid.'

Stella laughed, a welcome sound. 'It's the business of people like us to make it less so.'

I warmed at the 'people like us'. I did want to be a person like Stella, a person who embodied the spirit of Helen's Hope. Was what I had just done in the spirit of Helen's Hope, or was it reckless and high-handed? I decided not to mention it. The chances of Patrick actually finding his way back to Helen's Hope were slim, so what was the point?

'Look,' Stella said, and pointed across the park to a group of girls in navy coats. 'That's Miss Farrell's school, Ellis House.'

'The ones we made the curtains for? A girl from home goes there.' I was glad to have my thoughts distracted from Patrick Neill. I squinted hard at the group, who were walking in a shrubbery in twos and threes with a teacher, but it was too far away to see if Flora was one of them.

'I always wanted to go to boarding school.' I was about to tell Stella how much I enjoyed school stories but something stopped me. I didn't want to admit to childish tastes. Nor did I want to say I had invited this Miss Farrell to the open day. It had been a silly idea: as far as she was concerned we were just the lowly seamstresses who sewed the curtains for her dormitories.

The Ellis House girls were gathering in a clump, and the teacher was telling them something. Then they got into a line, two by two, and started to walk towards the gate. They would pass us and I'd be able to see if Flora was there. I felt glad to be here with Stella and not in a supervised group of girls being told where to go and who to walk with.

I wondered if they'd been to church and realised that for the first time ever I hadn't been to Sunday Mass.

The girls were approaching us now, a neat navy-blue crocodile. And my heart jumped because one of them was definitely Flora! She was walking with a short, roundish girl, and she looked bored, beating at the shrubbery with a stick. They came so close that I could hear every word the short girl was saying, all about what Miss Minnis had said and weren't the lower fourth beasts and had Flora noticed that Mabel – here the girl blushed – had told her to straighten her hat and did Flora think it meant anything?

'I suppose it meant your hat was crooked,' Flora said and went back to beating at the shrubbery. I could see how much she wished she were back in Mullankeen, cantering along the lanes on Moonshine.

She glanced at me and Stella as she passed us; I thought she looked envious of our freedom. I opened my mouth to say hello, to enjoy her surprise and delight at seeing someone from home. But her eyes slid right over me; she wasn't snubbing me; she just clearly had no idea who I was.

My heart gave a little squeeze of sadness. I had admired Flora Galbraith for so long, thought her so dashing, and now I saw her as a bored, cross, sad and probably lonely girl. Obviously she had nothing in common with her walking partner. I glanced at Stella; she was someone worth admiring, but now I knew she was starting to see me as someone worthwhile too, not just a firebrand, not just a troublesome big-mouthed kid.

'I used to want to go to boarding school,' I found myself telling Stella. 'I sort of wished Helen's Hope would be like one. But it's much better.'

Stella grinned. 'Glad you think that.'

'Did you like school?'

'I went to school in a Manchester back street and left when I was fourteen,' Stella said. 'I was always in trouble.'

'What for?'

'Oh! Too pushy, too outspoken, too challenging.'

'Me too! At least – well, the nuns just told me I would go to the bad,' I admitted.

'But you haven't.'

'There's probably still time,' I said and Stella laughed again.

'Stella?' I asked. 'D'you think some people just *are* bad? Like Fraser?'

Stella shook her head. 'He's a bully. But he's scared of this Uncle Alec character. And it must have been hard on him, losing his father. And I suppose he thinks what he's doing is right. For God and bloody Ulster.'

'He's a liar too,' I said. 'Saying that about Ivy.'

Stella bit her lip. 'There's some truth in it,' she said, and when I gawked in disbelief she said quickly, 'I know I can trust you not to tell. Obviously Cassie and Scottie know. And Brigid. I'm only telling you so you won't mention it to Ivy. But it's more or less true. Ivy was – well, what they call a streetwalker. Her father was killed at the Somme –'

'Like Fraser's.'

'And then her mother died.'

189

'Like ours.'

'Yes. But we were luckier. Ivy had no family. There was nobody to look out for her. She lost her job in the mill and then she found she could earn money by selling her body to men. More or less as Fraser said. She was fourteen, Polly, and men were paying her to – you don't need me to spell it out, do you?'

I shook my head.

'She was rescued by a charity – a mission that takes girls from the streets and tries to show them a different life. Cassie knows one of the women who runs it. Ivy was young and bright; they thought she'd do well at Helen's Hope.'

'She's not very popular.' I realised this now. Ivy was outspoken and fierce, and she'd been mean to Catherine when she identified that Catherine was weaker than her, but she didn't have proper friends. Not like me.

'Maybe she's scared of people finding out about her past.'

I remembered her collapsing when I destroyed the flag, and how Stella had stroked Ivy's hair and how jealous I'd been. I wasn't jealous now.

'I suppose Fraser knew her by reputation,' Stella said.

'Or recognised her. I wouldn't put it past him to –'

'Possibly. Which makes the way he threatened her even more disgusting. Double standards. Bloody men.'

'But all men aren't like that, are they? I mean, Sandy's not like that.'

'Absolutely not.' She smiled but it was a sad smile.

'Are he and Edith …?'

She didn't say anything for a long time. She finished her tea and looked at some blackbirds digging for worms in the flowerbed. Then she said, 'Sandy and Edith are very well suited. Very good for each other. Come on.' She stood up and brushed a few crumbs from her skirt. 'We should get home.'

Chapter 28

'CAN I go and see Ivy?' I asked Scottie after lunch.

'She's really not very well.' Scottie looked uncertain. 'But a visitor might cheer her up. Don't let her upset herself.'

Ivy was in bed in the room beside Cassie and Scottie's where patients were always put. It was a slip of a room with a tiny window. Ivy, in bed, looked small and white, her bandaged hand beside her on the pink coverlet. The cuffs of her nightie were frayed.

'Fraser knows it wasn't your fault,' I said, not bothering with small talk. 'I showed him the flag. We told him you'd worked night after night. He's absolutely one hundred per cent totally sure that it's not your fault. So you can stop worrying. He can't do anything to you.'

Scenes like this were common in books. Usually the girls were enemies brought together by a dramatic rescue. Ivy was the baddie who wasn't really bad, just unhappy – in the books the Ivy character often had a shady past, perhaps expelled from other schools or the daughter of a convict, but so far she had never been a reformed prostitute. I was the brave rescuer, wronged but generous. (I couldn't really say that Ivy had wronged me, except by teasing Catherine, but I knew now that life didn't follow the books that closely.) What Ivy had to do now was to burst into grateful tears and clutch my hand (I could do without that), and then Matron (Scottie) would lay her hand on Ivy's fevered brow and say, 'Her temp's down. She's past the crisis. You've saved her life.'

It wasn't like that. Ivy lay back against the pillow, looking cross. Her small breasts pushed against the thin fabric of her nightie. I tried not to think about the fact that men had given her money to have their way with her.

'You haven't got a clue,' she said. 'If I were you I'd go back home and never show your face round here again.'

'Don't be daft,' I said. 'This Uncle Alec might be angry with Fraser – but that serves him right for bullying you. He can't do anything to you. All you need to do is get better. You look awful.'

'Thanks.'

'I mean, you must be exhausted. All those nights. I'm sorry I destroyed your work. At least, not exactly sorry. I don't know. It was sort of beautiful. I just – it's complicated.' She looked at me coldly and I struggled on. 'It wasn't the flag itself. It was what it was going to be used for: to intimidate people. A show of –'

'Loyalty,' Ivy said.

'But that's not how I see it. Or how Catherine or Brigid or …' I didn't want to list all the Catholic girls and anyway I wasn't just talking about Helen's Hope. 'To us – to nationalists – it's a symbol of oppression. Especially since the election. Being waved in triumph. Rubbing our noses in it. It makes us feel excluded and –'

'So clear off over the border then.'

'Oh, Ivy! It's not that simple! You think the border's just a matter of drawing a line and keeping everything British on one side and everything Irish on the other? Think of how an Irish republican flag would make *you* feel. That's why they're both banned here. That's why Cassie wouldn't take Fraser's order.'

I thought of Patrick Neill, who had fought for that flag. This new Northern Ireland – would it look after men like him? Would it look after men like Leo?

I opened my mouth to tell Ivy that my own brother, a Catholic and a nationalist, had fought for that flag too, and how he had been treated for it, but Ivy had closed her eyes as if she had had enough of me. I gave up, left the room and went into the garden to finish my quilt, but mostly I sat and yawned. My disturbed night and busy morning were catching up with me. A morning-afterish mood had settled over the whole place. Girls were sitting in groups, chatting quietly. Brigid was playing piano with the window open, something romantic and sleepy. Catherine and Maisie were doing a jigsaw. Winifred and Agnes were sorting out a flowerbed that had been dented by some over-enthusiastic dancers yesterday. Tessa and Jean were having a passionate but good-humoured argument about who was dishier, Rudolph Valentino or Douglas Fairbanks.

Maggie joined me, unfolding her deck chair beside mine. 'Well?' she said. 'What's been happening?'

I'd missed Maggie. 'Is your headache better?'

'I'm fine. Not like poor Ivy; she's in bed sick. Where have you been? I was starting to wonder if there was something going round. Looks like Stella's in bed too.'

She jerked her head towards Stella's window. It was open, but the curtains were shut, swelling and billowing in the breeze. I knew Stella wasn't ill, but I imagined her lying down, feeling sad about Sandy and Edith. Maybe even crying again. Poor Stella.

'Oh, you know, around.' Stella hadn't needed to tell me that this morning's mission, and everything about Ivy and the flag, was secret.

'I was thinking,' Maggie said, 'about Edith's classes. Why shouldn't she extend them to some of the local women? Some of them can't read and write.'

'They don't have much spare time,' I said, 'and what about their children?'

'The children could do dancing with Brigid while Edith taught the mothers,' Maggie suggested.

I laughed. 'You're as bad as Stella for sorting out people's lives for them!'

'Or as good as?'

'Yes. It's a good idea.'

'It's one thing to put on a nice show for people; it's another to actually reach out and offer them help. It might make them value Helen's Hope – not just tolerate it.'

'Would Edith mind? She's got enough to do.' And she was probably getting married soon, but I didn't say that.

'They could join in with her regular classes.'

'Sandy could do gardening with the children.' If he stays. I remembered him saying he couldn't keep a wife on what he earned here. Of course, Edith could get a job and keep herself, she was clever enough – but married women didn't. At least, Mammy had helped in the shop, but it was different when you had a business. And women like Edith were too posh to go out to factories and mills. I wondered what had happened to her dreams of going to Queen's University. I looked round the garden, saw the girls in their groups, all mixed up. Not just Catholics and Protestants, but sewing girls and factory girls and college girls. The open day had been good for us in that way.

The June air was lazy; when I closed my eyes I could hear bees and somewhere, not far away, a thrush singing, so much gentler than the squabbling seagulls this morning. Catherine laughed, a warm bubble of sound. From beyond the wall, children shrieked, a dog barked, but the normal city noises – carts and motor cars and works hooters – were absent because it was Sunday. Tomorrow Sandy would set the factory back to rights and we could worry about not having enough work, but for now, as long as I didn't think about Leo or Patrick or Fraser or Ivy, for now, with Maggie beside me so dependable and kind, everything felt perfect.

I looked at my quilt. It was finished, the backing fabric stitched neatly. I would need to press it, and some of the seams weren't as straight as they could be, as higgledy-piggledy as the ragged hedgerows around Mullankeen, but it was pretty and bright and new and I had made it myself.

'That's lovely,' Maggie said. 'You'll be able to put it on your bed tonight.'

I looked forward to seeing it in the Lavender Room, to my bed being dainty and pretty. Only Ivy's would have a dull grey blanket now. I thought of Ivy as I'd just seen her. So low and worried. About the hard life she'd had. What it was like to be scared of people knowing what you'd done. How you couldn't just draw a line under your past and move on.

'It's not for me,' I said. 'It's for Ivy.'

'Ivy?'

'She doesn't have much,' I said, 'and she's not very well. It'll be a nice surprise for her.'

Maggie gasped.

'What?' I said. 'It's not that strange an idea.'

'Not that,' Maggie said. 'But talking of surprises...' She nodded at Sandy and Edith who had appeared from somewhere. They were talking to Cassie. I couldn't hear what they were saying, but Cassie gave a little exclamation and hugged first Edith and then Sandy. Then she grabbed Edith's left hand, and there, catching the light and glinting in the sun, was a small diamond ring.

'Look!' Maggie said.

'Oh!' Without thinking I said, 'So it's too late.'

'Oh, come on!' Maggie sounded shocked. 'Sandy's ten years older than you. You surely don't –'

'Not *me*.' I lowered my voice. 'Stella.'

'What about her?'

'Isn't it obvious?'

Maggie shook her head.

I wasn't going to gossip about Stella, so I just said, 'Oh, nothing. Doesn't matter.'

They stayed to tea, and everyone noticed the ring and buzzed about it. Tessa said she was in mourning and she hoped this didn't mean Sandy would have to leave Helen's Hope. Brigid sighed and looked at her own engagement ring. Catherine wondered if we would all be bridesmaids and what colour would suit her best. Ivy wasn't at tea, but Stella was, sitting beside Cassie. She looked as pale as Ivy had been, and ate little, but talked brightly, and I thought how brave she was. Courage wasn't just about standing up to people like Fraser.

Cassie stood up and tapped her glass. 'I have an announcement to make,' she said, and Tessa nudged me. 'Edith and Sandy,' she said.

But it wasn't; I guessed that Edith and Sandy would hate a public announcement; they were both quiet and reserved, and Cassie would know that. The announcement was about the opening of the Northern Irish Parliament on Wednesday.

'The King and Queen will be in Belfast for the occasion,' Cassie said, her voice very neutral, 'and for many of you, this will be a joyous day – the opening of our own parliament.' There were mutters among the girls, some approving, some clearly not. 'But you all know the trouble there's been. It's possible there will be violence on Wednesday. Those with nationalist sympathies are not at all happy about a Belfast parliament. Miss Scott and Stella and I have had a long discussion about the situation. We would prefer Helen's

Hope girls not to join the crowds to see the King and Queen.' She held up her hand when there was a babble of dismay. 'I said we would prefer it. Obviously you must make up your own minds. You are young women with minds of your own, not children. We have no objection to the parliament – we hope very much it will usher in a more peaceful and respectful dawn for our country –'

'It won't,' Brigid said.

'No, I fear you're right, Brigid. There is so much anger. Recent events have been worrying – bombing and rioting and sniping – and those poor people burnt out of their homes. Not an auspicious start for a new dawn. My personal worry is that there will be street violence on Wednesday and that some of you might get caught up in it. But you are not forbidden to go. You must use your own judgement. All we ask is that you are sensible.' She sat back down, looking anxious. Scottie gave her arm a reassuring pat.

I thought about Fraser and Uncle Alec. The flag had been for Wednesday, for the King's visit. Surely the local UVF would be able to get another one in time? It wouldn't be as special as the one honouring Fraser's father and his friends, but they'd have some kind of union flag to wave. But not one made at Helen's Hope. Because of me. Ivy's pinched, white face swam in front of my rice pudding. *If I were you I'd go home and never show your face round here again.*

But she was wrong. They couldn't actually do anything to me.

Chapter 29

'BACK to porridge,' Catherine said. She threw her stockings on to the floor and wriggled into her blue cotton nightie.

I retrieved the stockings and hung them over the back of Catherine's chair. 'It's felt like a holiday, this weekend, hasn't it?' I said.

'I can't stand the idea of that rotten college tomorrow,' Catherine said.

'Why don't you ask your mammy if you can go to a domestic science college instead?' I said. 'You'd love that.'

'D'you think she'd let me?' Catherine perked up.

'Ask her.'

Tessa yawned and rotated her shoulders. She picked up her comb and ran it through her hair. 'Anything would be better than putting the labels on lemonade bottles,' she said. 'Today's put me in the mood for a proper holiday. I might pop down and see the King on Wednesday.' She said it as if the King were a pal she might grace with a visit if she had nothing better on. 'I hope Ivy's all right by then. She won't want to miss it.' She frowned. 'You don't think she's got measles, do you?'

'No, I'd have noticed if Dr Scott had called.' Catherine did a pretend swoon.

'And we'd all be in quarantine,' I said. 'It's probably a bilious attack or a cold.' I didn't say I knew exactly what was wrong with Ivy.

'I wonder when Sandy and Edith will get married,' Catherine said. 'D'you think they'll invite us all?'

'Course not.' Tessa giggled.

'Can you two stop talking?' I asked. 'I'm tired.'

When I woke to a window full of orangey light my first thought was, *Again! Is Ivy mad? She can't be trying to make another flag!* She had looked so sick; surely she wouldn't have the strength to get herself down to the factory, let alone make a new flag from scratch. And what with? But maybe she was crazy enough – or desperate enough – to try. Well, I couldn't let her! I'd have to go and stop her. I wouldn't bother Stella this time; I'd manage on my own. I pushed back the covers and looked out the window towards the factory.

And screamed. Because that orange glow wasn't a light. It was flames. The factory was on fire.

Behind the windows flames danced, evil and orange. The door was black and blistering. When I opened my bedroom window I heard the crackle of flames and smelt a dark, acrid smell. The few yards between the house and the factory looked a very short distance.

I shook Catherine and shouted, 'The factory's on fire! I'm going to tell everyone.'

Catherine took ages to wake up, muttering and rubbing

her eyes, but Tessa snapped into action. 'Fire bell!' she said. 'Beside the front door. Run!'

I shoved my feet into my slippers and dashed across the landing and down the stairs. The house felt so normal and safe and quiet, nothing to suggest that only a few feet away a fire was raging. I grabbed the bell and clanged it as hard as I could. Its clamour filled the whole house – the whole street, surely!

Stella was first to appear, fully dressed, then Cassie, and then a stream of girls, puzzled or scared or both, hair standing on end or streaming over nightgowns or plaited for the night.

'What the –?' Stella demanded.

'Factory's on fire,' I said.

'Right. Everybody out the front,' Cassie said.

Scottie appeared at the top of the stairs, helping Ivy who seemed to be in hysterics. Cassie opened the front door, and everyone filed out, Stella counting them as they went. I stayed beside the door and did the same, because I knew how easy it was to lose count and two heads were better than one.

'Seventeen,' she said to me.

'I make it seventeen too.'

'But it should be eighteen!' Her face was tight with panic.

'No, Sarah went home yesterday.'

'Oh, yes! Thank God. Right, go and line up with the others on the front lawn.'

'Should we not call the fire brigade?'

'I'll see to that.' Cassie ran to the phone under the stairs.

'I'm going to check on the factory,' Stella said.

'You can't! You heard Cassie – out the front's safest.'

'Just a quick look.'

I followed her down the back passage and into the kitchen. I couldn't wait sedately on the front lawn if Stella was putting herself in danger. This was too much like a school story – the schools in stories were forever burning down. Stella flung open the back door. All the factory windows showed orange now and behind the orange the room was ominously dark with smoke. Even from the back door, across the yard, the fumes made us cough.

'Will it get to the house?' I asked. 'Shouldn't we – I don't know, throw water on it?'

'Or make a barrier?' said Stella. 'But there's nothing to do that with. It's not like we can dig a ditch. There's just an empty yard between the factory and the house.'

'Well, that means there's nothing to feed the fire,' I said.

'Air! Air will feed it!' Stella was all panic, her eyes huge, her face strained.

'But there's nothing to burn,' I reassured her, not that I knew much about the ways of flames. 'It will just die out – but it won't come to that,' I added, 'because the fire brigade will be here first. Listen.' Somewhere, not close, a siren wailed. But there were fires all over the city these days – who knew if this was coming to us?

'The machines will all be destroyed!' Stella cried.

'Machines can be replaced.'

'That's easy to say.'

'Stella,' I whispered, 'was it because of me?'

'How could it be?'

I remembered Catherine, back at home when I first heard she was coming to Belfast, saying *You always think everything's about you.*

'I cut up the flag. That's why they burnt the factory down, isn't it?'

The flames cracked and spat. It felt strange to be standing so close to them, but this didn't feel like a conversation we could stop. 'We don't know for sure,' Stella said.

'Ah, come on! It's obvious.'

'Yes, you cut up their flag. But I insulted them. Ivy tried to appease them. And in the first place, Cassie dared to set up Helen's Hope with all sorts of girls from all sorts of backgrounds ... here in bitter old Belfast. How far back do you want to go? There's no excuse.'

'Maybe we shouldn't have provoked them.'

'So are we meant to creep around in fear forever? Scared to annoy anyone? Scared to make our voices heard? Scared to live the lives we want – lives that aren't hurting anyone?' Her voice was soft and fierce, her face lit up by the flames across the yard.

'I don't know.'

'This new parliament – I'd like to believe it was going to create a fair society here, where everybody's respected, but I just don't think it's going to happen.'

'But the men in the parliament aren't like the people who did this! I read in *The Belfast Telegraph* that the new administration could be, er' – I tried to remember – 'trusted to give the same rights and privileges to all classes and creeds.'

'So they say. But they've also said a Protestant state for Protestant people, and the nationalists are boycotting the parliament. That doesn't bode well. And the border – and what's happening in the south; it's a proper war down there, far worse than here – it's all just a mess. I can't see any hope.' She sounded so bleak. 'I can't see any hope for anything.'

I couldn't bear to hear Stella like this: Stella who was always so positive. Maybe that's why I felt cheeky enough to say, 'You're probably feeling low because of Sandy.'

'I beg your pardon?'

I gulped, but I had to keep going. 'Um – I thought you might be sad that he and Edith ...'

'Why would I be?' Her voice was fierce.

'I thought – maybe – you sort of ...'

'What?'

'Loved Sandy,' I said timidly. My face burned, and I didn't know if it was embarrassment or being so near the fire.

To my surprise Stella gave a dry sort of laugh. 'Sandy?' she said. 'No, of course I don't love Sandy! I mean, I do, in a way – he's my best pal. But I don't *love* him, not like that.'

And then I realised what I'd been too stupid to see.

'Edith?' I breathed.

So it wasn't only girls in stories who fell in love with other girls. Real girls could too. And Stella was too old for it just to be a pash, like I had had on Flora and now had on Stella. Maybe one day I would fall in love properly.

Before Stella could respond, there was a crack from inside the factory and a volley of sparks reddened the windows.

'We need to go round the front,' I said. This was no time to be thinking about love! 'Cassie will be wondering where we are; you don't want her to worry.'

'But so many of our hopes are in that building.' She sounded as savage as the flames, and part of me knew why she couldn't bear to leave it. The fire was destructive and furious. But because we knew it couldn't actually hurt anyone, there was a kind of ghastly beauty in it.

'Helen's Hope isn't just a building,' I said. 'It's a spirit. And the factory is only one part of it. What matters are the people, and they're all out the front, and they need *you*, Stella. To calm them down and, well, just be with them. Come on.'

I felt very adult, and calm, and sensible. I held my hand out to her, and after a moment, to my surprise and relief, she took it. We turned our backs on the flames and went to join the other girls.

Chapter 30

ROUND the front of the house was like a different world. A world of people and concern. Arm round my shoulder. Cup. Warm in my hands. The smell of cocoa. Someone crying.

'Polly. I thought you were dead.' The crying person was Catherine. She hugged me to her until I had to fight her off to get some breath.

'Don't be daft. You nearly made me spill my cocoa. We were only looking.'

'Was it scary?'

'Yes,' I said, though scary didn't quite fit how it had felt, watching the factory burn. 'If it had been the house, instead of just the factory ...'

Catherine hugged me again. 'Don't even say that.'

'There you go,' said a voice I didn't recognise. I looked up to see a neighbour – Hubert's wife. She held out a rug to me. 'Take this, dear.'

I wasn't cold, but I took it to please her and actually it was comforting.

'It's desperate altogether,' said the woman beside her. 'Trying to kill wee girls.'

'It doesn't matter to us what yous are,' said another. 'We've never had burnings round here and we don't want to start.'

They drifted off with their blankets. I looked at Stella who was beside me again. 'What are they talking about?'

'The fire. You know people – Catholics – have been burned out in other parts of the city. I suppose it's starting round here now. And they started with us.' She shuddered.

'Not just Catholics,' Maggie said.

'Mostly Catholics.'

'Stupid to target *us* then. Sure there's as many Protestants here as anything else.'

I struggled out of my cocoon of rugs. 'The fire brigade are here!' Maybe there was still time to save the machines. Maybe the building could be saved from total destruction.

'They took their time!'

'They'd other fires tonight.'

I looked round the scene in front of Helen's Hope. Girls huddled in blankets, shivering and scared and shocked. And somewhere, not far away, someone was glad about this. Had caused this. Had made and thrown a fire-bomb of some sort. Were they disappointed that nobody was killed? Or had they just wanted to scare us and that's why they'd thrown their fire-bomb into the factory, where they wouldn't expect anyone to be? The only thing I knew for sure was that this wasn't simply because there were Catholic girls at Helen's Hope. It was more complicated than that.

It would always be more complicated than that.

But it wasn't only a scene of fear and distress. The women from the street were out in force, carrying trays of steaming tea and cocoa, blankets over their arms. I heard offers to bring girls home with them for the rest of the night. Promises to turf children out on to sofas to let our girls have their beds. They seemed to like us better, to accept us more easily, when they had the chance to help us. Men were talking about the work that would be needed to secure the factory. To mend it, if it could be saved. Father Byrne was there, talking to the Reverend Hamill. They were shaking their heads. They looked very alike.

Two firemen came out of the front door and talked quickly to Cassie. She nodded and said to us all, 'Sergeant Grant tells us that the fire is out. The factory's badly damaged but the house is safe. We can all go back inside, you'll be glad to know. Just keep the windows shut at the back of the house.'

A muted cheer rang out from the girls. Cassie stepped forward. 'Can we just thank our neighbours?' she said. 'They've rallied round like – well, like real neighbours. Three cheers!' And the cheers rang out loudly in the smoky air.

We were making so much noise that at first we didn't notice the third fireman. The one who, his face grey under its smears of soot, came up and said to Stella, 'Miss? Can you tell me who's in charge here? We've found a body in the ashes.'

Chapter 31

THE factory stood blackened and gutted at the end of the yard. Maggie and I were standing looking at it in the cool morning light. Of all of us, we were the ones who had known Corporal Patrick Neill best – not well, probably nobody had known him well since he got back from France, but we were the ones who had invited him to Helen's Hope.

And I was the one who had given him the factory key.

'It's not your fault,' Maggie said for the hundredth time. 'It's the fault of those …' She tried and failed to find a word. She shook her head.

'I feel like I lured him to his death. He must have been so desperate. So lonely.'

And Stella and I had stood and watched, unknowingly, as he had burned to death. I hadn't even remembered that I had given him the key. I had been too preoccupied with Stella. With myself. I swallowed, seeming to taste the acrid black smoke mixed with bile and last night's cocoa. I had been struggling not to be sick ever since we had been told that the body found in the factory had been identified as that of Corporal Patrick Neill, of no fixed abode.

'You were kind to him,' Maggie said. 'You only wanted to help. You'd no idea something like this would happen. How could you?'

'I'd completely forgotten him! If I hadn't persuaded Stella to leave, we might have seen his face at the window or – or something. Or was he already d-dead by then? Was he burned to death or overcome by smoke?'

My teeth chattered against my lip and I bit hard to make them stop, adding the metallic tang of blood to the sickening taste in my mouth. I retched.

'You have to stop this,' Maggie said, giving me a brisk sideways hug. 'It's not doing any good.'

'If I'd known.'

'Nobody could have known.'

But I couldn't help thinking I should have. I knew how angry Fraser and his friends were. I knew how much I'd provoked them by destroying their flag – how Helen's Hope provoked them just by daring to exist. I read the papers. I knew people were burned out and intimidated; I just hadn't expected it to happen here. I hadn't really expected Patrick to come to the factory. I'd given him the key to make *me* feel better, and then I'd forgotten all about him.

'You were kind to him,' Maggie said again. 'That's the important thing.'

'He's dead. That's the important thing.'

And I turned away from her. Nothing she said could help. Catherine was especially kind to me too, offering to give me her blue glass bracelet, but I shrugged it off. 'I don't want it,' I said, and went off to walk on my own.

THE King's visit to open the new parliament came and went. I didn't read about it in the papers and as far as I knew nobody from Helen's Hope went.

Stella came to me and said there were plans to rebuild the factory, and a group of girls was going to set up a committee to discuss the future of Helen's Hope.

'I'd like you to be part of it,' she said. 'People listen to you. You have good ideas.'

A week ago it would have meant so much to have Stella look at me with respect, to be invited to take part in the future of Helen's Hope. But I couldn't think about the factory without imagining Patrick Neill meeting his lonely death there. I remembered Stella, the night of the fire, saying she couldn't see any hope for the future. I felt exactly the same.

'I don't think so,' I said. 'Ask someone else.'

Stella hesitated. 'Look,' she said, I know you're upset about what happened to Corporal Neill. We all are. It was ...' She shook her head to show that she had no words. 'But you can't wallow in it. You have to – well – buck yourself up a bit.'

I stuck my chin in the air. 'I'm not *wallowing*. What would you know?'

'I know about getting on with things when you don't feel like it,' she said. I remembered Edith and Sandy. But that was only love. Nobody died.

I'd never felt this bad in my life. I'd grieved, of course, when Mammy died, and I'd felt afraid of Leo and mourned the loss of the old Leo. I'd been bored and angry and lonely. But I'd never had this crushing weight that pounced on me the minute I opened my eyes every morning, settled on my shoulders and wouldn't shift.

Walking was the only thing that helped a bit. There was no sewing to be done, of course – it would be weeks before the factory was on its feet again – and though we weren't exactly encouraged to go out alone, nobody stopped me when I crept down the stairs in the early mornings, usually after a night of tossing and sweating, waking every hour from choking dreams. I would walk the streets round Helen's Hope, sometimes catching the sharp tang of smoke on the dawn air and wondering who else had been burned out. Graffiti scored the walls.

ULSTER IS BRITISH. UVF. FENIANS OUT

I would see the shipyard men on their way to work, leaving their houses in ones and twos, then joining others on the street, until by the time they reached the main road there was a dark stream of them, like the crocodile of girls I had seen from Flora's school, only many, many more. My eyes were gritty with exhaustion, my stomach churned constantly and my legs shook with lack of sleep and food – my throat closed when I tried to eat – but I couldn't stay home. I needed to try to walk off the restlessness, the horror and the guilt.

One morning, as I shrugged into my frock, I heard a moan from the bed beside me.

'Go back to sleep, Catherine,' I whispered. 'I'm only going for a walk.'

'You're crazy,' Catherine said, stretching her arms behind her and opening her mouth in a huge yawn. 'Why do you do it?'

'It helps.'

'You're as bad as your Leo.' She snuggled back down in her pillow and was asleep again before I had buckled my shoes.

But she made me think. Leo. Leo walked like this, restless and haunted. Leo couldn't sit still. I had never understood, never even tried to. Leo was fine, I had reasoned. The war hadn't got him. The flu hadn't got him. Why couldn't he just be grateful? Buck up a bit, as Stella had told me?

Why couldn't he draw a line under the past and get on with his life?

Why couldn't I?

I slipped out of the dorm as usual, across the landing and down the stairs. As usual I went to the front door and slid aside the big bolt that was always put across at night. As usual it creaked and shuddered in my hand as I tried not to make too much noise. But before I had pulled the bolt right across I stopped, crossed the hall again and went through the kitchen. I let myself out of the back door and stood in the cool grey morning, looking across at the factory. I made myself stand and look. Someone had died there. Someone who might well be alive today if I hadn't put an idea in his head. I would never forget him, and I would never forget what had happened to him.

But I had to stop blaming myself. And I had to work hard to stop it happening to other people.

I didn't stay outside for long. I went into the common room and found some paper and a pen and before I could change my mind I wrote a letter.

Dear Leo,

I know you'll be surprised to hear from me, and I'm sorry I haven't written before. I'm sure Daddy has told you what happened here. It was a shock to all of us, and I think it's helped me realise how difficult things must have been for you. Maybe when I come home we could go for some walks together. I hope you are doing all right.

Your loving sister, Polly

P.S. I'm sorry – I should never have said what I did. I didn't mean it.

It wasn't much. A few lines on a page. Wobbly and awkward perhaps, blurry and smudged in places, but a start.

Chapter 32

STELLA said of course it wasn't too late to join the group to discuss the future of Helen's Hope.

'The group's grown,' she said. 'Everyone wanted to join in so we're meeting in the front room.'

The window was open and anyone walking down the street could have looked in, but maybe that was a good thing. From the open window you could hear children shrieking in the street. I was fairly sure it was Queenie I heard singing 'I'll Tell Me Ma'.

Cassie and Scottie took their places at the front, and the rest of us found seats where we could, crowding onto settees and grabbing cushions to make the floor comfier.

'So,' Cassie said. 'We've had some good news. The insurance is going to pay for the factory to be rebuilt. It will take time but it will be good as new. If we want it to be.'

'If?' Stella asked.

'As you know, the factory hadn't been paying its way. And unless we get a big order we might have to cut our losses.' She looked round us all and sighed. 'We've lost more girls this week.'

Winifred and Mary had gone home, scared to stay in streets where Catholics seemed so unwelcome.

'We can't give up,' Stella said. 'The fire showed us who our enemies are, but we knew that anyway. But it also showed us we have friends. Look at how good the neighbours were. And there's talk of a treaty between England and Sinn Féin.'

'That won't help things up here.'

'It might. If it ends the war down south, there'll be some kind of peace.'

Brigid looked unsure. 'I don't think –'

But she was interrupted by the doorbell.

'See?' Stella said. 'There's not a day now a neighbour doesn't call on us, asking for help filling in a form, or bringing an apple pie or something. Polly, would you –?'

I sped to answer the door, glad of something to do. I still had to work hard to keep my mind off Patrick and Leo. I hadn't had a reply to my letter.

The porch was mostly glass so I could see before I opened the door that the visitor was Mauve Hat.

'Good afternoon,' she said. 'Is Miss Cassidy in?'

'Well, yes, but she's in a meeting,' I said, 'but please come in.'

I wished someone else had opened the door. I wasn't sure where to take her, but guests were normally shown into the sitting room, so I supposed I should do that. When we went in, Cassie stood up at once.

'Miss Farrell!' She sounded pleased. 'Girls, this is Miss Octavia Farrell, from Ellis House.'

Most of the girls looked blank but Brigid said, 'Oh, yes, the school we did the curtains for.'

So that's who she was!

'And a jolly good job you did on them,' Miss Farrell said. 'Which is why I've come in person to ask if you'd take on – well, rather a bigger task.' She beamed round the room, her hat bobbing.

'Oh, dear.' Cassie looked sad. 'I'm so sorry, but – haven't you heard our bad news? Our factory was burnt down. We'd need to restock with new machines. It could take months to get the place up and running again. I'm afraid we can't possibly take on –'

'It's not so much sewing,' Miss Farrell said. 'Though when you are up and running again, I'd like to talk to you about making our uniforms.'

'But what else could we …?'

Miss Farrell looked round the room. 'Not only is the standard of work from Helen's Hope excellent, but I fully endorse the spirit of your enterprise. I was most impressed with what I saw on your open day. I was thrilled to be invited.' Cassie and Scottie looked blank, and a tiny bubble of satisfaction rose inside me. 'And the young women I met were a credit to you – resourceful and kind.'

'Mauve Hat,' I whispered to Maggie and she squeezed my hand and grinned.

'It was always my dream to have a really good school,' Miss Farrell went on. 'One where girls would learn so much more than the curriculum can offer. Tolerance and understanding and social awareness. Your community at

Helen's Hope is so diverse. So equipped for the challenges of the modern world. My girls could learn a great deal from you.'

Cassie and Scottie exchanged delighted glances.

'This young woman here.' Miss Farrell gestured at Stella. 'I've seen you speaking at Labour rallies.'

Stella, unusually, blushed.

'I was most impressed. I wonder if you would be prepared to come to Ellis House and teach classes in political economy and citizenship. For a proper salary, of course.'

I imagined Stella striding into the classroom, bossing all the navy-blue girls and opening up their minds to feminism and internationalism and new ideas. I wondered if Mauve Hat – Miss Farrell – knew what she was letting herself in for!

Stella laughed. 'I'm not a qualified teacher.'

Miss Farrell waved that aside. 'You know enough to teach my girls, believe me. Heads full of nonsense, most of them. Ponies and hockey.'

I thought about Flora Galbraith and wondered how she would take to political economy.

'I'm so busy here,' Stella said.

'Yes, but, Stella, a lot of what you do is basic clerical work,' Cassie said. 'Maggie would be more than able to take that on.'

Maggie bit her lip with pleasure and I joggled her arm, grinning at her delight and the thought that she would certainly be staying at Helen's Hope for the foreseeable future.

'Well, then I'd love to,' Stella said.

'Splendid. I'll add it to the prospectus for next year,' Miss Farrell said. 'Now, if I could just have a quiet word with you, Miss Cassidy?'

'Certainly.' Cassie stood up. 'Let's go and have tea in my study. My partner, Miss Scott, will come too. Stella – you're more than capable of keeping things going here.'

The three women left and we all looked at each other in glee.

'Surely,' Stella said, 'with this to keep us going, we could run classes for the local community. Reading and writing. Gardening.'

'Dancing,' Brigid said.

'Even if there's no room for dancing, we could do music and singing.'

'We could have a regular girls' club!'

'I'm going to learn self-defence,' Stella said. 'Jiu-Jitsu – it's all the rage in England. And then I can teach that too.'

'Hooray!'

'I could teach the penny whistle,' Ivy said. It was the first time she had spoken. She had been subdued since the fire, apart from when she'd seen the new patchwork quilt on her bed, when she had stared and then actually hugged me. I couldn't say I liked Ivy, but I was glad I'd given her the quilt.

'I could help her,' Tessa said. 'And Catherine – you could easily teach them what you learn at that old domestic science college you're going to.'

Catherine had written home to ask if she could go to domestic science college, as I had suggested, and Auntie

May agreed. She was starting in September, after spending the summer helping Scottie in the kitchen at Helen's Hope, and she was delighted with herself.

She blushed. 'Oh, posh girls like that won't need to learn to cook,' she said, but she looked pleased all the same. I tried to imagine Flora Galbraith learning to bake scones. Well, perhaps she would like it better than political economy.

Brigid spoke up. 'Martin and some of his old shipyard friends have the skills to help rebuild the factory, once we get the go-ahead. It would be just the thing for them.'

Mention of her Martin made me think of Patrick, but this time not just with sick guilt and despair but with the determination to make Helen's Hope really work, to help make a society of mutual respect and tolerance, where people like him couldn't fall through the cracks. Because there wouldn't be any cracks.

'I'm going to write to the insurance company this instant,' Stella said. 'Make sure they know how important it is to get us sorted out as soon as possible.' She looked determined and Amazonian again, and I guessed that she would get over her feelings about Edith by throwing herself into her work. She grinned round at us. 'Well,' she said, 'I started this meeting feeling very flat. But now it seems we have a lot to look forward to after all.'

'With confidence,' Maggie said firmly.

'Well, with hope anyway,' I said, and we all cheered so loudly that it was some time before I realised the doorbell was ringing again. I slipped out to answer it.

Through the frosted glass of the porch I saw it was a man, a man with his back to me. A back that seemed familiar and yet ...

It couldn't be Sandy – he wouldn't ring the bell. We weren't expecting Dr Scott. I pulled open the door.

He turned. And I knew why he had seemed familiar. 'Hello, Leo,' I said.

Dear readers, we hope you have enjoyed reading *Hope against Hope*. The following pages contain an interview with the author, Sheena Wilkinson, in which she discusses writing this book and two related books: *Name upon Name* and *Star by Star*.

Little Island

An Interview with the Author

Sheena Wilkinson

This is the third of a trio of historical novels: Name upon Name, Star by Star *and* Hope against Hope. *Did you set out to write three books about Irish history?*

Hope against Hope is a stand-alone novel: you don't need to have read *Name upon Name* or *Star by Star*. But I love it when writers create a world where you meet old friends in a new context. When I finished writing *Name upon Name* I wondered what had happened to the characters, especially Sandy, whom I had always loved. When I was asked to write *Star by Star*, I decided to include some of the same characters so that I could find out! Similarly, *Hope against*

Hope brings back Stella and Sandy and even Edith and Miss Cassidy – minor characters I always cared about. I felt terrible about killing Helen off in *Star by Star*, even though it was right for the story, and being able to honour her memory with the hostel being named after her felt like I was making up for that in some way!

Why set a book in 1921?

After writing about the Easter Rising of 1916, and the General Election of 1918, 1921 was the obvious choice. There was so much going on, in particular the partition of Ireland. Because of Brexit, the UK border in Ireland has once again come to the forefront of political discourse. I grew up with army and customs checkpoints and closed roads, with so-called 'bandit country' and no-go areas, but in recent years I have enjoyed being able to cross the border freely, often hardly being aware of it. The threat of losing that freedom terrifies me, and I wanted to write a book that showed people living with the very early days of that border.

Polly is quite different from Stella and Helen. Do you have a favourite heroine?

That's like asking a parent if they have a favourite child! I have a soft spot for all three heroines, and I'm glad they contrast with each other. Helen very much shared my feelings of alienation as a child in Belfast, not belonging to either 'side' of the cultural and political divide, and I loved being able to write about those feelings. Stella, the heroine of *Star by Star*, is more like how I *wanted* to be: she is very feisty, which I was, but I've always admitted that she was much kinder than I was – and very much braver. One of my best friends, Susanne, who's always my first reader, has said she thinks Polly is the heroine who's most like me, which intrigues me!

I suppose she is like me at fifteen in some ways – she wants to do the right thing, but she's often held back by fear and self-consciousness. She's also very imaginative and wishes she could make reality more like stories – which is exactly the way I was, and still am to an extent. I had great fun writing about her love of school stories, which I share, and her frustration that Helen's Hope, and the real city and country which surround it, just don't measure up to her fantasy worlds. When I was younger, growing up on a Belfast housing estate during the Northern Ireland troubles, I used to wish I was at the Chalet School in Austria, or having adventures with Laura Ingalls on the wild prairies, or galloping a horse over the Essex fields in *Flambards*.

The Great War ended in 1918, but it still seems part of everyday life in 1921. Are you a bit obsessed with that war?

Yes, the war ended in 1918, but of course you couldn't just draw a line under it – its impact on individuals and thus on society carried on for a very long time. If I wrote a book set in 1931, never mind 1921, those effects would still be felt. It takes Polly a long time, and some bitter experiences, to be able to understand how the war has affected her brother, Leo. The characters of Sandy and Patrick also help her to understand him. I became an adult just as the Northern Irish Troubles were coming to an end, but their impact is still felt today, so I've always been interested in the aftermath of conflict.

Is it hard to write books set in the past? How do you do your research?

I love writing historical fiction, and the early twentieth century is my favourite period. I can spend hours reading and going to museums, until there comes a point when I need to just start writing the story. I especially like considering what life was like for girls then, and how it has changed. It is easy enough to find out the facts, but what's harder is to get people's attitudes right. You need to do more than stick a longer dress and an old-fashioned hairstyle on a character to make her convincing as someone born in, say, 1906, like Polly. You need to think about what she would have known and believed. For example, Polly is confused about the feelings she has for some other girls, but she doesn't think about that in the way a modern girl might – she wouldn't have that vocabulary. I read a lot of novels written at the time, which are great for giving you insights into people's attitudes. I also love reading the newspapers of the day, though you end up with very sore eyes – the print is tiny!

Is Helen's Hope based on a real hostel?

Helen's Hope is imaginary, but in the early twentieth century there were indeed hostels for working girls in most cities. They tended to be run by religious charities and were much stricter than Helen's Hope! Some forward-thinking people around that time were starting to think about alternative ways of living, which is why I thought of Helen's Hope as more a kind of community than an ordinary hostel. The cross-community element of it, and the fact that there are girls from different social classes, makes it a target. Sadly that's based on fact: many people are suspicious of those who want to break down barriers. I saw this growing up in Northern Ireland, which remains, even today, a very divided society.

So what's next?

Who knows! I've definitely got the historical fiction bug, and I'd love to write about the thirties or the fifties or sixties. After all, there's no decade when there wasn't something big impacting on young people's lives. I'd love to see what happened to the next generation of Irish girls. Helen can't have children because she's dead, and I don't imagine that Stella will, but maybe Polly or Edith could appear in a later book as the heroine's mother.

ACKNOWLEDGMENTS

Writing a novel set in 1921 Belfast was the biggest challenge I have set myself so far, and as always I am grateful for the guidance and support of the wonderful team at Little Island who helped me make it what it should be, and to my lovely agent, Faith O'Grady, who has looked after me for ten years now.

Thanks to the Linen Hall Library, Belfast, which as always was where the bulk of the research took place.

Hope against Hope would probably never have been commissioned without the success of 2017's *Star by Star*. Thank you so much to all the festival organisers, librarians and teachers who gave me the chance to talk about 1918 all over Ireland and the UK. And a special thanks to Booktrust for naming it a 'Future Classic' – what a wonderful boost that was. As always, I feel deeply thankful for the support of the children's book community in Ireland, especially to the brilliant people at Children's Books Ireland.

The Royal Literary Fund has been by my side for several years now, and their practical and moral support make all the difference. Writing can be lonely, and I'm forever grateful to have so many wonderful, funny, clever writer friends who know what to say to keep me as sane as someone who makes things up for a living ever can be.

My family and friends have all been as great as ever: special thanks to Susanne who is always my first and most enthusiastic reader and who never tires of talking about my made-up characters. Julie McDonald cast her wise history-teacher's eye over the Historical Note: thank you!

And finally, to Seamus, my own Hope: all my love.

Sheena Wilkinson
Castlewellan
November 2019

ABOUT THE AUTHOR

Sheena Wilkinson is one of the most acclaimed Irish writers for young people. Since the publication of the multi-award-winning *Taking Flight* in 2010, she has published several novels, including *Grounded*, which won the 2013 Children's Books Ireland Book of the Year award. Her first historical novel, *Name upon Name*, set during the 1916 Easter Rising, was chosen as Waterford City's 'One Community, One Book' title; *Star by Star*, set at the time of the momentous 1918 General Election, when women in Ireland voted for the first time, won the 2018 Children's Books Ireland Honour Award for Fiction and was selected as a Booktrust 'Future Classic'. Sheena lives in County Down, where she spends her time writing, singing, and walking in the forest thinking up more stories.

ABOUT LITTLE ISLAND

Based in Dublin, Little Island Books has been publishing books for children and teenagers since 2010. It is Ireland's only English-language publisher that publishes exclusively for young people. Little Island specialises in new Irish writers and illustrators, and also has a commitment to publishing books in translation.

www.littleisland.ie

Little Island